Harlem
SUMMER

2³

Harlem
SUMMER

23

by

WALTER

DEAN

MYERS

SCHOLASTIC INC.
New York   Toronto   London   Auckland
Sydney   New Delhi   Hong Kong

Cover and book design by Elizabeth B. Parisi.

Copyright © 2007 by Walter Dean Myers.
Cover illustration copyright © 2007 by Shane W. Evans.
All rights reserved. Published by Scholastic Inc.
Printed in the U.S.A.

ISBN-13: 978-0-545-34235-3
ISBN-10: 0-545-34235-X

6 7 8 9 10   23   20 19 18 17 16 15 14

A REGISTERED LETTER BRINGS BAD NEWS FROM THE SOUTH AND I START LOOKING FOR A SUMMER JOB — HOPEFULLY, NOT IN A FUNERAL PARLOR.

I like Harlem in the summer except when it gets too hot, which it had been for the last week and we hadn't even reached July yet. On my block, women sat in their windows and kids hung out on the fire escapes trying to catch whatever breeze got lost and wandered up to Harlem. Old Man Mills and Jimmy Key were sitting on the stoop playing checkers. Jimmy had been wounded in the war and walked with a cane that he held across his lap as he studied the board. Everybody, except maybe Jimmy, knew that Mr. Mills was going to win.

"Man, it is some kind of hot out here," Mr. Mills said, as he jumped two of Jimmy's men. "Little while ago I saw a dog get up from where he was lying under a tree to get a drink of water from that leaky hydrant down the way. But what surprised me was that his shadow didn't get up and go with him. It stayed right under that tree where it was cool."

"I'm thinking of getting me one of those new electric iceboxes," Jimmy said. "If I get one I'm going to keep the door open and sit right in front of it all day."

"I heard that some rich folks got two or three of them refrigerators in their house so they can have a cool glass of water in whatever room they're in," Mr. Mills said. "That's what you call high living."

"I still don't see why you need an electric icebox when all it does is make the same kind of ice that the iceman brings," Jimmy said.

"Don't pay him no stead, Mark." Mr. Mills turned toward me and jerked his thumb toward Jimmy. "He don't realize this is 1925. He's still living back in the old days when they used to feed Christians to the lions and whatnot."

"This conversation don't have a thing to do with no Christians and lions," Jimmy answered. "It's okay being modern but you can't let it go to your head. That's what's wrong with that teacher down in Tennessee talking about how people come from monkeys. He's trying to be modern but what he's talking about don't make a bit of sense."

"I read in the paper where they interviewed a monkey and asked his opinion on the subject," Mr. Mills said.

"Now you know you lying, Mr. Mills," Jimmy said. "Nobody asked no monkey nothing!"

"The monkey said he didn't know if any humans came from monkeys," Mr. Mills went on, "but the way some humans acted, no self-respecting monkey would admit to it if it was true!"

They went on with their checkers game and Mr. Mills won, just as I knew he would. They were starting a new game and I was sitting on the bottom step when the mailman came and asked if anybody knew the Purvis family.

"I guess they got a mailbox in the hallway like everybody else," Mr. Mills said.

"Somebody has to sign for this letter," the mailman said, wiping the sweat from the back of his neck with his fingers.

"They live in apartment 4-S," I said. "Go on up."

He backed away from the stoop, looked up at the building, and called out "Purvis" as loud as he could. Nobody answered him and he sucked his teeth and started into the building.

"Now that guy has got a good job," Jimmy said. "He shouldn't have any complaint going up a few flights of stairs!"

I could hardly wait for him to come back downstairs so I could go up and see what was in the letter. Both Mr. Mills and Jimmy knew the letter was for my family but you just didn't take a letter you had to sign for without thinking about it.

When the mailman came down I asked him if he had found the Purvis family but he was huffing and puffing so much he didn't even answer me.

When I got upstairs the door to our apartment was open and I walked from the hallway into our kitchen and saw my father sitting at the table with his head down.

"Benny, this is terrible!" Mama was saying. "What are we going to do?"

Daddy looked like he was going to say something, but then just threw his hands into the air and dropped them back down into his lap.

"What happened?" I asked.

"We just got a letter saying that the land we had down in Currie was sold for back taxes," Mama said.

She was crying so I knew it was serious. Still, I hadn't heard anybody talking about moving down to North Carolina so it didn't bother me that much.

"Maybe he can work part-time," Daddy said.

"We told him we were going to pay for his first year," Mama said. "That's the crucial year. If they can make it that first year they usually make it all the way through. You know Reverend Powell was saying that in church."

Now I knew what they were talking about. The big deal was my brother Matt's going to college. He had been accepted at two colleges, Storer in West Virginia, and Livingstone in North Carolina. He had decided to go to

4

Storer, and Daddy was going to sell the land in Currie to pay his tuition.

"Now what are we going to do, Benny?" Mama stomped her foot but I knew it wasn't going to do any good. Daddy wasn't making much money working at Connie's Inn as a handyman and had lost his part-time job cleaning the Cotton Club when it was closed down for violations. I felt bad for Daddy because he was always catching it from Mama's side of the family, the Carters. Connie's Inn, on 131st Street and Seventh Avenue, was not a low-life place. Some of the best musicians in the world played there, including Fletcher Henderson's band. Since prohibition, when they passed the amendment to the Constitution that stopped the sale of booze, nobody got too drunk there, either.

"Your father isn't dumb," Mama always said. "He's just relaxed more than a man ought to be relaxed if he's living in Harlem, New York City."

My father was relaxed and I liked that. Mama's family was always on the go. What the Carters wanted was to run the world, or at least the Colored part of it.

"Maybe I could sell my life insurance," Daddy said, knowing full well Mama would have a snitsy fit over it.

"Nobody in my family is going to go out of this world without enough insurance to bury him." Mama was wiping her hands on her apron. "Now how would I look with you laying out in the parlor and don't even have a coffin. Benny, what is wrong with you?"

"I'm just trying to think of something to do," Daddy said. "So Matt won't be too disappointed."

My brother, Matt, was the big deal of our family. The way my mama had it figured, he'd be the first Harlem Purvis to go to college. He had just turned eighteen and had made great grades in his senior year at George Washington High School. Mama made it clear that she thought he was the best thing going, and Matt believed every word she said. He was sort of stuck on himself and that was okay with me because we didn't hang out or anything like that. It wasn't that I didn't like my brother — okay, maybe I didn't like him that much — but it didn't matter because, as Mr. Mills said, some folks were upper-crust and some were plain old crumbs. I was more crumby than crusty.

The thing was, I wanted Matt to go to college, too. If he went to college then I would have our room to myself. Also, if he went to college maybe Mama would be satisfied and I wouldn't have to go. What I wanted to do was to play saxophone with a jazz band. Music was just naturally in my blood and that was all there was to it. I knew Mama didn't appreciate that, but one day, when I made the Big Time, she would understand just how I felt.

I tuned back into the conversation and heard Daddy saying he didn't know what to do, and Mama was saying that the whole family had to pull together to raise the money for Matt. She told me to go to the corner store and call Uncle Cephus and tell him what had happened. I said I would because you didn't tell Mama "no" when she wanted you to do something, but I did not want to tell no Uncle Cephus what had happened.

C. Cephus Carter owned the House of Palms Funeral Home over on Lenox Avenue, down from Freddy's Fish Shack. Now, whenever you talked to that man he only had one thing on his mind, and that was how good the undertaking business was.

"Everybody you see is a potential customer!" he liked to say. And he said it again and again and again. "People dying today ain't never even thought of dying before!"

I knew he was going to suggest that Matt forget about college and get into the undertaking business with him. I went down to Mr. Peterson's Candies and Sundries store, looked up Uncle Cephus's number in the phone book, and dialed it. When I got him on the phone he said that the loss of the land was God's way of telling Matt to do something else with his life instead of just wasting it sitting in some classroom learning how to wear a coat and tie.

"That's how God does things!" Uncle Cephus said. "He just ups and does what He knows is right."

A cat came into the store and rubbed against the radiator and I stuck my tongue out at him.

"The Lord works in mysterious ways," Uncle Cephus went on. "His wonders to perform! Now isn't that wonderful?"

The cat rolled his eyes at me just as I was telling Uncle Cephus it was truly wonderful.

He was saying that he would drop by the house later, when I saw Edie walk in and put a dollar on the glass counter that held the candy. I was *not* in love with Edie Waller but I did think about her a lot. She had two things going on in her favor. Number one, she was kind of cute, even though she was pretty big for a girl; and number two, her brother, Fats, played at the Lafayette Theater and made records with a professional record company. Fats with a sax was what I wanted to be. He could play a mean piano and an even meaner organ. Maybe that's because his father was a preacher. Fats played jazz. He could swing with anybody, and even bang out some classical music that sounded righteous. More than that he was an okay guy and full of fun. So, I didn't love Edie, but I was very interested in the young lady who was, at sixteen, exactly my age and the sister of Fats Waller.

"Edie, how are you?" My smooth line.

"Oh, hello, Mark." Edie had a big, open smile and opened it all over me. "Did you see my brother today?"

"No."

"He's looking for two guys to help him load some trucks over in New Jersey," she said. "Something like that. So how you doing?"

"I'm doing good," I said. "He still needs somebody to help him?"

"He mentioned there's five dollars in it," Edie said, pointing to the candy she wanted. "He's over at the Lafayette now. You can catch him there if you hurry."

The Lafayette Theater was only a few blocks away and I went right over. I had spoken to Fats a few times and recognized him as he was coming out.

"Hey!" I said.

"Hey right back at you." Fats pointed a huge finger at me. "What you up to?"

I told him what Edie had said and he told me that some guy had hired him and Crab Cakes Dean to bring a load of cologne from Union City, New Jersey, over to Harlem. He asked me if I wanted to make five dollars cash money. As I said yes I got a funny feeling in my stomach. You didn't make no five dollars in one night unless you were doing something a little on the shady side. But I figured it couldn't be too bad because Fats was no more crooked than anybody else. I figured I would just do the unloading like Fats said, and then later I would just mention, in a casual kind of way, that I wouldn't mind playing with him sometime.

He told me when he was going to need me and we agreed to meet at the corner of 126th Street and St. Nicholas at eight o'clock. He asked me if I could get another guy. I knew I could. I was thinking about my main man, Uptown Henry Brown.

HOW THE RUINATION OF MY WHOLE SUMMER STARTED AND I BEGAN TO BE A NEW NEGRO WHEN I WASN'T REALLY THROUGH BEING THE OLD NEGRO I USED TO BE.

All of Mama's relatives were a little on the snooty side, and her sister, Aunt Carolyn, was just as bad as her brother, Uncle Cephus. She came over the next morning and said that she knew all about how Daddy had lost the land down south. She said that I should stop by her job at the 135th Street YMCA and maybe she could get me a summer job. Mama called me out of my room to say good morning and asked me wasn't I thrilled that Aunt Carolyn was looking out for the family. All the while Aunt Carolyn was sitting at the table looking all pleased, her lips stuck out like she was holding a strawberry in her mouth.

"Yes, ma'am."

Soon as I had passed around enough "yes, ma'am's" and arranged to go over to the Y in the afternoon, I went out and tracked down Henry Brown. Henry was my Friend to the End, the Ace of the Race, the Mighty Black Who's Got My Back. We planned one day to make a record on the Black Swan label with Henry on guitar, our friend Randy Johnson on piano, and me on sax which would make us all richer than J. Pierpont Morgan. We had first met in the fifth grade in P.S. 157. I was in the school yard pinned up against the wall by Long-headed Willie Spruill, who held me with one hand while winding up his fist to drive me through the wall of the handball court with the other. Henry came up to us and told Long-headed Willie that he'd better be careful because my cousin had just got out of jail and was just looking for somebody to shoot. I didn't know where he had heard that before but it worked. Long-headed Willie gave me a shove but he didn't beat me up. Me and Henry had been friends ever since.

Henry was going over to the East Side, where the Italians live, to buy some new strings for his guitar. He said that he and Randy had practiced together over at Randy's house and had come up with a new name for our trio: The Fabulous Three.

I said it was all right but I really didn't think it was that good. I told Henry about Matt and the whole land down south bit and how I was going to look for work to help out. I also ran down the job with Fats and the cash money that went with it.

"Whose mama I got to kill for them dollars?" Henry asked.

"You ain't got to kill nobody's mama," I said. "But if we're working with Fats it's got to be good."

Everybody knew who Fats was. Lots of people could play but Fats had already made a record for Okeh Records and was the most famous young dude we knew. I was still a little worried about the job but I knew if me and Henry got in with Fats, life could switch to the fast lane in a hurry.

So at 1:30 I fell into the YMCA and checked out Aunt Carolyn. She was small, just about five feet, and the color of Hershey's chocolate — not the bar, but the hot chocolate when you put milk in it. She dressed nice, too. She always had something special about her, like the way she pronounced each word so careful you thought she was worried about breaking it. She was from my mother's side of the family and really a lady. When I arrived at the Y she was wearing a regular blouse and skirt, but she also had on a long necklace made of shells from Africa.

"What do you want to do with your life?" she asked when I sat at her desk.

I said I did not know what I wanted to do with my whole life but maybe I would drive a truck like my friend Henry's father. She didn't have a comeback for that but she wrinkled up her mouth and her forehead at the same time so I knew she wasn't thrilled about my choice. I didn't say anything to her about the saxophone or the trio because she was just like Mama when it came to music. If you weren't playing church music, or la-de-da opera stuff, she thought you were low-down.

Aunt Carolyn had two job openings. One was for a cleaner at the Renaissance Ballroom. The pay was $14.50 a week and free lunch. But Aunt Carolyn said that it didn't make sense to spend my time cleaning a ballroom when I could be learning a trade.

I could walk to the Renaissance Ballroom and I knew some hot musicians hung out there, so I told Aunt Carolyn that I didn't mind cleaning or sweeping floors because it kept the blood circulating and the internal organs healthy.

"Where did you learn that nonsense?" she asked.

"From the guy who has that little table in Blumstein's," I said.

"The man who wears a dirty brown robe and calls himself the Prophet of Profit?"

"Yeah."

"And he's the one you've chosen to lead you to the Good Life?"

I asked Aunt Carolyn about the other job. It was all the way downtown, at 14th Street. *The Crisis* magazine needed a Bright Young Man to work in its advertising department and paid $14.00 a week, but they only wanted me for four days. That sounded all right, but just all right. It paid more than the cleaning job but it would cost me five cents to get downtown every day and five more cents to get back uptown to Harlem. But it was still better than working with Uncle Cephus in his House of Palms so I said I would take it. Aunt Carolyn said it was a good choice because the magazine was one of the Leading Intellectual Journals of the Negro race. That didn't sound too good, but I said I would go anyway. Aunt Carolyn told me to see someone named Jessie Fauset on Thursday.

Thursday came and I headed downtown wearing a suit jacket and a tie even though it was so hot I was sweating before I got to the elevated train. There were two overhead fans in the car I was on and neither of them worked. Half the people on the train were reading their newspapers and two guys were talking about Babe Ruth getting fined. I was reading the *Amsterdam News*, the best Colored newspaper in New York. If anything happened in Harlem you had to wait until Thursday to find out about it in the *Amsterdam*. I saw where Bill "Bojangles" Robinson was going to play a benefit at the Lafayette Theater. I was probably the only one on that subway car who knew about it.

The Crisis was on Fifth Avenue and 14th Street. You couldn't miss it because there was a big sign in the windows. I wondered how they could see out onto the busy street below. When I asked the elevator operator if he knew

Jessie Fauset he didn't answer, just pointed into the elevator and I got in. He took me up to the fifth floor, opened the door, and pointed out. I made a mental note not to like him.

Just about everyone I saw working in the office was black. There were a few light-skinned people there who might have been Colored but I wasn't sure. They were some very serious-looking people. All the men wore white shirts and ties, and all the ladies looked prim and proper. I looked around the place and it seemed all right, but nothing special. There were fans in the corners but they weren't making it any cooler. I watched two women typing and saw them wiping the sweat from their faces. One of the women asked what I wanted and I told her I'd come to see Mr. Jessie Fauset about a job.

"*Miss* Fauset is the lady near the window," the woman answered, smiling.

If they ever put Colored people on wedding cakes they could have used *Miss* Fauset as a model. Everything on her was in place and neat-looking. She had one little drop of sweat on her upper lip and she flicked it off with one finger before she started to ask me questions.

"What are your career goals?" she asked.

She didn't look like she knew anything about jazz so I said I wanted to be a teacher because she looked a little like a teacher.

She asked me if I could be on time every day and remember to wear a tie to the office. I said yes and then she went and talked with a man while I filled out a job application that asked questions about where I lived and what colleges I had attended.

After a lot of whispering and a lot of looking over their shoulders at me, Miss Fauset came back, looked over my application, and said that I was hired. I had to report to work Monday morning at 8:30.

"We at *The Crisis* magazine represent what is being called the New Negro," Miss Fauset said. "Dr. DuBois has said that the Negro race, like all races, is going to be saved by its exceptional people. We are trying to make sure that we promote and encourage that talented ten percent of black people so that they will be able to lead us. This ten percent is the core population of the New Negro."

"That's very good, ma'am," I said. I didn't know who or what she was talking about.

When I got home I told Mama and she said she heard that *The Crisis* magazine was published by the National Association for the Advancement of Colored People. Matt chimed in and said that they were for the advancement of the Colored race and against people getting lynched. From what they were saying I figured the job was a big deal. Still, I wished I didn't have to wear a jacket and a tie to work.

Miss Fauset had looked really pleased to be telling me

about the New Negro, but I didn't get the feeling that she thought I was one. But I wasn't going to get my mind messed around with anything that was going to keep me from my music and making a good impression on Fats Waller. Working for Fats was a lot more important than anything I had ever done before, and a lot more important than being whatever a New Negro was.

We can't just jump up and ask Fats if we can play with him," Henry said as we stood outside of the Apollo Theater. "I think we should just say that we'd like to play at the Apollo. That way he'll know that we play and then he'll ask what we play. I'll tell him you blow sax and I wail on guitar, then we can just ease on into us playing together later."

"Yeah, but I want to play with him now," I said. "So maybe we should tell him that we were thinking about making a record."

"You think we're ready to make a record?"

"I've heard some of the Black Swan records and they're pretty good," I said. "You know what might be better is to ask him if we can get together in September."

"Whoa — and then we can practice over the summer!"

That sounded good to me. My dad had met Mr. Pace, the guy who owned Black Swan Records. I didn't want to tell Henry just yet, but I was sure we were on our way.

"Hey, is that it?" Henry pointed to a big green truck that had stopped on the other side of the street.

The crosstown trolley rolled slowly by and I tried to look through the windows to see if anyone was getting out of the truck. When the trolley had passed I saw Fats standing on the sidewalk looking over toward the Apollo.

Fats was wearing a suit jacket and a tie that was loose around his neck. When he saw me coming toward him he grinned that big grin of his and I smiled back.

"On time!" Fats pointed a big finger at me and made a face. I was so happy and excited I could have peed root beer.

"Hi, Fats." I shook his hand. "This is my friend Henry."

Fats beckoned to the guy who was driving and he got out of the big Mack and came up to us.

"Crab Cakes, these are my good friends Henry and Mark," Fats said. "Mark here is a little sweet on my sister, Edie, and maybe there's a song there somewhere."

I extended my hand toward Crab Cakes and he grabbed it and pumped it and then reached for Henry's hand and did more of the same. "You got a dog?" he asked.

"No, I don't have a dog," I said.

"You like dogs, huh?" Henry asked, giving me a look.

"I like my dog, Abby," Crab Cakes said. "I raised her from when she was firstest born. She couldn't even keep her eyes open."

"That happens sometimes," I said.

"We all ready to roll?" Fats pointed to the truck.

Henry and I both said yes. Crab Cakes got into the driver's seat, and Fats squeezed into the cab with him. Fats said there was plenty of room in the rear.

Two minutes later me and Henry were sitting on the floor of the truck bumping along 125th Street. Henry didn't say anything but I knew he was mad. The ride was breaking us up. We were bouncing off the truck floor like two black-eyed peas on a hot griddle and nowhere near enough to Fats to talk to him.

We rode fifteen minutes or so and then we heard the engine cut off. I could smell the river and when Fats hollered into the back of the truck that we had a while to wait before the ferry came we got out.

"I'm going to get something to eat," Fats said. "You guys stay with the truck."

Henry didn't say anything but I could tell he was still mad by the way his lips stuck out. We were at the 48th Street ferry terminal. It had grown cool and I felt a few drops of rain. I was having second thoughts about the whole job. I wiped the sweat from inside my collar as Crab Cakes came to the back of the truck and started talking about his dog again.

"I got her when she was about one day old," Crab Cakes said. "First thing she saw when she could see real good was me."

"That's good," Henry said. "She's home waiting for you now, right?"

"Naw, she's down home in Baltimore." Crab Cakes snorted twice, hunched his shoulders up and down twice, too. He was a small dude, maybe nineteen or twenty, and a little bug-eyed. "Down on North Central Avenue. You know where that is?"

"No."

"I live there all my life," Crab Cakes said.

"Go-o-o-d," Henry said, giving me a poke with his elbow.

Crab Cakes was a little weird. It wasn't just that he was talking about the dog, it was the way he kept hunching his shoulders when he talked and glancing around as if he was looking for somebody.

"You play an instrument?" Henry asked Crab Cakes.

"No, I got a dog," was the answer.

"Go-o-o-d," Henry said again.

It was 9:00 and we just sat there waiting and sweating, mostly sweating, until a little past 9:30 when we saw Fats coming back. He brought a bag of doughnuts and passed them around. Then he told us to get back into the truck and soon we were moving onto the ferry.

I had crossed the river on the ferry before, but never inside a truck. I think it would have been all right if I was in the cab. The smell of the water was good and the ride on the ferry was easy. A seagull landed on the tailgate and looked in at me and Henry with its head cocked to one side.

"This is not exactly the way to fame and fortune," Henry said.

"It's the way to five dollars and getting in with Fats," I said.

"Yeah," Henry said, wiping the sweat off his face with his shirttail, "him and this dude's dog."

Crab Cakes didn't seem to be as bright as me and Henry so I figured that Fats must have hired him because he could drive, or maybe because he was strong. Either way, he was getting in the way of us talking to Fats.

The ferry didn't take long and soon we were riding in New Jersey.

The roads in New Jersey were even worse than the ones in New York. When we heard the engines cut off I was sore and mad. We got out and I saw we were in an alley somewhere. A short white man came out and spoke to Fats. Then he came over to me and Henry and gave us the once-over. He looked like a tough guy.

"Bob Auerbach," he announced, looking us over.

"Henry Brown." Henry stuck his hand out but the white guy didn't shake it.

"You boys get the crates on the truck as fast as you can," he said. "I don't want to be here all night."

There was a loading platform and me and Henry went into the warehouse where there was a mountain of crates. Mr. Auerbach stood by the door and counted the wooden crates as we took them out to the loading platform where Fats and Crab Cakes were putting them on the truck. There was another white guy sitting in a corner with a shotgun across his lap. Henry took one quick look at the guy and rolled his eyes.

I was flat-out scared of guns and I kept my head down and didn't look around too much. What I was thinking was that maybe the crates that we were taking out of the warehouse had been stolen. Maybe *we* were even stealing them. The crates were marked WILDROOT HAIR TONIC and they weren't too heavy but there were a lot of them.

Henry and I were dripping with sweat when we got the last crates loaded. There was just enough room for us to squeeze into the back. Mr. Auerbach came and looked inside the truck.

"Don't let them shift around too much," he said in a gravelly voice.

Either Fats or Crab Cakes closed the back flap and in a

moment, hot, tired, and with almost no air to breathe, we were bumping along again.

"Yo, Mark, we stealing?" Henry's voice came out of the darkness.

"If we don't know what the deal is we can't be stealing," I said. "If the police stop us we'll say we were just hired to load the truck."

"What you think Fats knows?"

"I don't want to know what Fats knows because then I'll know more than I want to know," I said. "And when I saw that guy sitting in the corner with that shotgun I knew right then that I didn't want to know anything."

The ride back took exactly forever. I could tell when we drove onto the ferry because I could smell the water. When we were rolling again I didn't hear much traffic and wondered where we were headed. I was getting nervous and Henry had moved right into his whiny voice so I knew he was nervous, too. When the truck finally stopped and the back opened, it was Fats. At first I didn't know where we were but then I saw that we were on 126th Street and St. Nicholas Avenue.

"What time is it?" I asked.

"Quarter past two," Fats answered, pulling one of the cases down.

"We going to unload the truck?" I asked, knowing I was already going to catch it when I got home.

"I don't know," Fats said. "Right now we just got to wait here a while. How you doing?"

"I'm roasted through," Henry said.

"I'm going to sit in the cab and look out for our connection," Fats said.

"Hey, Fats." I was talking funny because my mouth was so dry. "You know me and Henry play with a band. You ever hear of The Fabulous Three?"

"No, I haven't," Fats said. "Maybe one day you'll invite me to one of your sessions."

"Yeah, sure," I said.

Fats went up toward the front of the truck and leaned against the front fender. When he was leaning against the truck that way you could see just how big he was, which was enormous.

We waited for another fifteen minutes and then a dark car pulled up behind us. Two white guys got out and came over to us. Fats came to the back and told us to hand down a crate. They opened the crate right there on the street and pulled out two bottles of liquor. One of the guys, a small dude with a pinched face, took the top off one of the bottles, sniffed it, and handed it back to Fats.

"Just drive it up to the garage and leave it there," he said.

"Will do," Fats said.

"Ain't your crew kind of young?" Pinch-face asked.

"Yeah." Fats nodded and rolled his eyes. "And they ain't lost their wonderfulness yet!"

"I'm Henry Brown," Henry said, offering his hand.

The guy ignored Henry's hand but peered closely at him before turning and starting back toward his car.

The car moved around us slowly, and Fats was already stuffing some of the bottles into his coat pockets.

"When are we getting paid?" Henry asked.

Fats pulled some money out of his shirt pocket and paid us each the five dollars we had been promised. He pulled the tarp closed at the back of the truck and told Crab Cakes to take it up to 138th Street.

"The same place we picked it up," he said.

Me and Henry were both glad to see that truck roll off.

"So when we going to get together?" I asked Fats.

"Sooner than that!" he said. "I got to hear you boys blow!"

Fats walked with a side-to-side swing. He was so big he looked funny waddling down the street.

"You think he's really going to come hear us play?" Henry asked.

"We practice steady and by Christmas we're going to have a record starring Fats Waller and The Fabulous Three," I said.

■ ■ ■ ■ ■ ■ ■ ■ ■ ■ ■ ■ ■ ■ ■ ■ ■ ■ ■ ■

I HAVE TROUBLE GETTING UP IN THE MORNING TO GO TO WORK. I HAVE TROUBLE ON THE JOB. I HAVE TROUBLE GETTING BACK UP TO HARLEM. AND THEN THE REAL TROUBLE BEGINS.

■ ■ ■ ■ ■ ■ ■ ■ ■ ■ ■ ■ ■ ■ ■ ■ ■ ■ ■

When I got home Mama was up and started in yelling at me about how she had carried me in the womb for nine months and how I wasn't even grateful. Then she woke Daddy up and told him that his worthless son had finally come home. Then she started yelling at him for not saying nothing and how he didn't care if I turned out to be nothing but trash.

"Why don't you ask him where he's been?" Mama yelled at Daddy.

"Where you been?" Daddy asked.

"Ask him if he was with his hoodlum friends," Mama said.

"You been with your hoodlum friends?"

"Why you asking him that, because you know if he was out doing dirt he ain't going to tell the truth!"

Daddy said something about there wasn't no use asking

me if I was going to lie anyway and Mama got all over him about that. When I went to bed they were still arguing but it was better than Mama yelling at me.

Mama woke me up in the morning by shaking me and screaming in my ear that it was the third time she had called me.

"Now you don't have time for breakfast!" she said when I got my feet over the side of the bed. "Do you have money for a sandwich?"

I remembered the five dollars and nodded. She gave me a mean look and left with a *humph!* I looked at myself in the mirror and it was not a pretty sight. Eyes half closed. Pajamas buttoned wrong. A little dried something on my cheek. I rinsed my face with cold water and looked again. No better.

By the time I had finished washing up and getting dressed, Mama had made toast and handed me a piece as I headed toward the door. The Third Avenue elevated train rocked and shook its way slowly downtown and I decided that any work that started this early could not be right for me.

Exactly one hundred and three billion people seemed to work around 14th Street and they were all jammed up coming out of the station. A clock in a store window showed that I still had three minutes to go before I was late.

I met Miss Fauset in the lobby and we took the elevator

upstairs. The staff of *The Crisis* was just finishing up the July issue and I watched as Miss Fauset pasted up copies of the stories on what she called a dummy board. Everything was checked twice.

"Dr. DuBois does not tolerate mistakes," she said.

I found out that Dr. W. E. Burghardt DuBois was the head of the magazine staff, and it soon was clear to me that nobody messed with him. Miss Fauset was the literary editor, and a woman named Effie Lee Newsome ran the children's section. I asked Miss Fauset if I would be doing pasting and she said probably not. I would be running errands, taking material to the printer, and checking the ads.

She wanted me to take several back issues of the magazine home and read them carefully. She also gave me another magazine, *The Survey Graphic,* to read. I wondered if I was going to be paid to do all of this reading.

Miss Fauset told me to start looking through the magazines and to find the works of people like Langston Hughes, Arna Bontemps, and Countee Cullen.

"These are *very* young and *very* talented writers," she said.

"They the New Negroes?" I asked.

"Yes, they are." Miss Fauset's eyebrows went up. "And they're very exciting."

She went over to her desk, pulled out a photograph, and then came back and laid it in front of me.

"Langston Hughes!" She said it like I was supposed to fall out or something.

I looked at the dude and saw that he had two eyes, a nose, and a mouth like everybody else, so there didn't seem to be anything new about him. I could only see one ear but I figured he had the other one so I didn't ask about it. I liked Miss Fauset though, so I didn't want to look as if I wasn't knocked out.

"He does look a little new," I said.

That gave her a little smile and I was glad I had lied.

My first official job at *The Crisis* was to go through the advertising section and compare it to the invoices from the previous month, to make sure we had not left anybody out. It certainly wasn't hard work but it was boring and it was hot.

The fans in each corner of the large office did two things: First, they pushed the hot air in your face. Then they made a little whirring noise as they turned slowly back and forth like they were trying to hypnotize you. Every time the fan pushed another little hot breeze into my face, my eyes started closing. I had to stand up just so I wouldn't fall asleep.

I looked around at all the other people in the office. They looked busy and interested in whatever thing they were doing. Miss Fauset said I was to go to lunch at twelve o'clock and I kept looking at the clock. The red hand went around and around but the others barely moved. I had to work to look away as long as I could and guess how much time had passed. Working was definitely not all it was cracked up to be.

For lunch I went to a diner on 15th Street that the office boy, Aussie Farrell, told me about. Me and Aussie had to go to lunch at different times in case someone wanted one of us to run an errand. I bought a pastrami on rye and an RC Cola. That was twenty-three cents. In Harlem you could have got the same pastrami and same RC Cola for fifteen cents.

The afternoon went by as slowly as the morning and I found out that I could actually fall asleep standing up. Everything in the office moved in the same rhythm as the fans except, of course, for the clocks, which moved slower and slower and slower. . . .

"It isn't going anywhere," Miss Fauset said when she saw me looking at the clock. "You don't have to watch it."

"Yes, ma'am."

By the time I was ready to go home I had a whole bag of books and magazines I had to read. Miss Fauset said I was going to love reading them and discovering what was going on in the black world, but it didn't seem that exciting to me. I lived in Harlem and I figured that was about as black as you could get without being in Africa.

The ride uptown was terrible. There were more people on the train and they were stinkier. I got home and started reading right after supper. I got through five pages of *The Souls of Black Folk* and started falling asleep. It was all about this heavy-duty drama stuff that sounded like school stuff except that it was black people. Then I had a great idea. I was going to tell Henry we should call ourselves The Hot Three instead of the Fabulous Three because that would make people think of The Hot Five, Louis Armstrong's group. I could practically hear us, with me playing sax like my man Buster Bailey sitting on a two-burner stove on a hot night, and Henry tearing up the strings, and Randy playing the ivories like Jelly Roll Morton — with our own business cards and everything. Or if I could get Randy to switch to clarinet, then Fats could play piano. That would be Groo with a capital V. Grooo-vy!

My brother was going out with this girl named Lavinia and they came tip-tipping in and soon they had parked themselves in the parlor, and Matt got his nerves swoll up enough to ask me to get her a glass of water. I told Matt that he was not a doctor yet and sure didn't have any servants running around and if Miss Lavinia wanted a glass of water I would point her toward the kitchen. Matt called me a plebeian. I told him to spell that out and when I look it up it had *better* not be anything bad.

Mr. Reece came by after supper, looking for Daddy, who had already taken off his shoes for the evening. When Daddy took his shoes off and "freed his bunions," he usually didn't put them back on again, not even for an extra job.

A lot of the jobs in Harlem were pickup jobs, just for the day. If you wanted to work for a moving company, you lined up on 126th Street and St. Nicholas Avenue. But if you wanted a pickup job at any of the clubs or cabarets, you had to see Mr. Reece. He and Daddy were good friends and when anything came along he let Daddy know. He came by after supper and said that two of the busboys were going to be out sick at Connie's Inn. Daddy asked Matt if he wanted to earn some extra money and he said no. Matt already had a summer job in an office on 136th Street and said that he had a lot of things to do for his boss in the morning. Mama was fixing to go out, putting on some face powder, but she stopped long enough to tell Daddy she didn't want Matt working in any club, anyway.

"Honey, we are black folks," Daddy said. "When we get a knock on the door it ain't no job, it's somebody looking for the rent. Folks in Harlem who want to eat can't be that particular."

"A doctor is particular!" Mama said, ending the discussion.

Mama left and Daddy was taking the jar of lemonade out of the icebox for Mr. Reece when I told him that I could use some extra money and would help clean the club.

"I see you waited until your mama left before saying anything," Daddy said. "But you can still go."

All the best musicians played at Connie's Inn. Me and Daddy and Mr. Reece started off together down to 131st where the club was located. It didn't take us very long and we got up there just as they were setting up the tables for dinner.

What they wanted me to do was to go around between the nightclub acts and pick up the dirty dishes. They had black waiter suits in the back, and I tried a couple on before I found one with a waistline small enough and the legs long enough to fit me.

The crowd started drifting in around eight o'clock and then really picked up at nine. That's when the entertainment started, too.

The first act was a chorus line, dancing to a tune called "I'm Just Wild About Harry." The girls wore short skirts that stuck out from their waists and black ribbons on their arms. They were looking mighty good and moving those big legs right on the beat.

"You ain't here to check out the girls," said Pete, the head of the busboys. "You clean tables eleven to twenty and if you get any dirt on a customer the cleaning bill is coming out of your pay."

I should have punched him in his face but since he was about six inches bigger than me and uglier than a baboon's butt on Monday morning, I let him slide.

Around midnight, Daddy came over to me and told me that a famous white piano player named Jimmy Durante had just come in. I looked around for him and saw him sitting with another white man and two women. The guy had a nose big enough to play a tune on.

I worked for four hours, until 1:30, and made almost two dollars in tips. All the time I was working I watched the saxophone players and listened to them carefully. What I liked was the way they made everything look so easy. They never squeaked or missed a note. That's the way I wanted to play. I could imagine myself playing as good as them and even better. Maybe I would play something really fast, something jumping and have everybody standing up clapping, or maybe I would play something slow, like "Always" and have people in love holding hands or looking into each other's eyes. Then when I saw I was getting to them, I would look over at Fats and he would nod and roll his eyes. Yeah.

Me and Daddy got to our house, and Edie was sitting on the front steps.

"What are you doing out this late, girl?" Daddy asked.

"I had to see Mark," Edie said softly, her head down.

"Mark, you didn't do nothing to be ashamed of, did you?" Dad looked at me out of the corners of his eyes.

"No," I said.

"Well, you walk Miss Edie home and get right back here."

Soon as Daddy went inside I asked Edie what was wrong.

"Fats told me to tell you that Crab Cakes is gone," she said.

"So?"

"So? What you mean *so*?"

"What do you mean?"

"I mean that crazy fool drove off with Dutch Schultz's truck, and all the liquor y'all got from Jersey," Edie said.

"That truck belonged to Dutch Schultz?" I asked, hoping I had heard wrong. Dutch Schultz was only the most notorious gangster in New York City.

"Yes, it did," Edie said. "And he's talking about all of you owing him a thousand dollars and how he's going to have one of my brother's fingers cut off for every hundred dollars he ain't got."

"I don't have his liquor, Edie," I said. "And I don't even know Crab Cakes. I just met him the night we got the stuff from New Jersey."

"You also met Dutch Schultz that night when y'all

37

came back." Edie squinted her eyes up. I remembered the pinch-faced dude. "And he met you. So you better start looking for Crab Cakes, that truck, and that whiskey or all of you are going to be in big trouble. You hear me?"

"That don't make no sense because I don't have any money to give anybody," I said.

"You got fingers and things he can cut off, ain't you?" Edie asked.

That's not what I wanted to hear.

■ ■ ■ ■ ■ ■ ■ ■ ■ ■ ■ ■ ■ ■ ■ ■ ■ ■ ■ ■

I START OFF HAVING A BAD DAY, MISS NEWSOME TEACHES ME WHAT UPPITY REALLY MEANS, AND THEN THINGS GET MUCH WORSE AS HENRY AND I LEARN THAT WE ARE DOOMED.

■ ■ ■ ■ ■ ■ ■ ■ ■ ■ ■ ■ ■ ■ ■ ■ ■ ■ ■ ■

Thursday and the day started off really bad. Miss Fauset told me to open the mail and I got a paper cut from the second letter I handled. It was terrible, right across the knuckle. I had a hard knot in my stomach from thinking about what Edie had told me about how Dutch Schultz was going to cut off her brother's fingers. What I was really wondering was what he was going to do to me. I had read a lot of stories of the gangs killing people and dumping their bodies in the river. That was mostly in the white newspapers, but in Harlem everybody knew that Dutch had a bunch of small businesses and he hired black people as well as white. It wasn't that he was all right but a job is a job when you needed one bad enough. I guessed that having your fingers cut off wasn't as bad but it wasn't what you would call good, either.

Miss Fauset asked me if I owned a dictionary and I told her no. She gave me one that had all the pages but the cover had fallen off. She told me I could take it home.

I looked up *plebeian*. It didn't look that bad.

When I got home, Mama was trying to get Daddy to take her to see *The Gold Rush* with Charlie Chaplin but Daddy said he was too tired to go all the way downtown.

Henry came by right after supper. He asked me if I had talked to Edie. He was whispering and I just nodded. Mama asked him if he wanted anything to eat and he said no. He asked me if we could go downstairs and sit on the stoop.

"I told Dutch Schultz my name and he was looking me right in the face!" Henry said as soon as we got outside. "Fats is almost famous. We're just nobodies. Dutch Schultz is going to smoke us!"

"He doesn't know my name," I said. I hadn't meant to say that — well, I must have meant to say it because it came out of my mouth, but I didn't mean to say it in a way that would mess with Henry.

Henry gave me a look and it was a sorrowful look that made me think he was going to cry.

"Okay, so maybe he's just going to kill *me* and throw *me* into the river," Henry whined.

"We need a plan," I said. "Something that's going to get us off the hook."

"Like joining the army?" Henry asked.

"The way I see it is we can do one of two things," I answered. "The first thing is to find Crab Cakes and the liquor and bring it back."

"You know where he went?"

"No."

"Edie said she thought his family lived in Baltimore," Henry said. "I've never even been to no Baltimore, and I'm not about to go there now and start asking around for no Crab Cakes."

"Then we'll just have to raise the money ourselves," I said.

"Ourselves? What about Fats? Crab Cakes was his friend, not ours. And Fats has a job."

That was true. Fats had told us all to leave the truck with Crab Cakes and had even taken some of the whiskey himself. Anyway, he was older than us, at least twenty and, more important, he could make twice as much as me and Henry combined.

Mr. Mills and Tim Kelly came up the street and I saw that Mr. Mills had his checkerboard under his arm.

"Boy, what you sitting there looking like a no-tail dog in a flea factory for?" Mr. Mills said, easing his tall frame down onto the stoop.

"I got a question for you, Mr. Mills," I said as he put the checkerboard on the top step and opened it up. "Say

41

that somebody was driving a truck with something in it that belonged to a gangster. And the truck disappeared with everything in it. Do you think the gangster would do anything to the people that just loaded the truck and didn't even know what they were loading?"

"Who the gangster?" Mr. Mills asked.

"I got the red pieces." Tim Kelly pointed to the ones he wanted.

"Dutch Schultz," I said.

Mr. Mills looked up at me and shook his head slowly. "What was in the truck?"

"We don't even know," Henry piped up.

"What was in the truck, son?" Mr. Mills asked again.

"Bootleg whiskey," I said.

"Yeah, he'd kill you," Mr. Mills said. "It wouldn't be nothing personal though. That's just the way things are done in the bootlegging business. You mess up and you get yourself kilt. Of course a lot of people don't mind dying. That's why they mess around people like Dutch in the first place. Anytime I see somebody hanging around the corner where he has his hangout I figure it's somebody who don't mind dying too much. You know what I mean?"

"Yeah."

Friday was my day off and I hung around the house all day feeling sorry for myself. I put on a record, King Oliver's

"Chimes Blues" and tried to play along with it but I was sounding so moany I put my sax away. Saturday and Sunday were both nice, sunny days, but I kept getting the feeling it was going to rain any moment.

Wrong! Back at work on Monday, Aussie, the mail clerk, was messing with me. He was older than me, but I guess he thought I couldn't fight. I couldn't fight against guys with guns, but I could deal with my dukes. If I had put my mind to it I could have been the black Jack Dempsey.

"You play any sports?" he asked.

"I play some baseball," I said.

"I could strike you out with my eyes closed," he said. "You don't look like you do nothing."

"I'm mostly a musician," I said, feeling the heat getting to my face. "I blow sax."

"Sax ain't serious," Aussie said. "I play drums. That's because I get into my African roots real deep."

"Sax ain't serious?" I looked at the slick-haired dude and felt like giving him one upside his head. "Yeah, I can see you're into your African roots. You must be from the Cango area."

"You mean Congo, chump."

"Naw, I mean Cango," I said. "'Cause you're one of those stink-breath dudes who can go around shooting off their mouths when they don't know what they're talking about."

He stood up and came toward me and I stood up and took a step toward him until we were chest to chest.

Miss Fauset came running over with her eyes bugging out and breathing through her nose.

"What are you people doing?" she asked. "This is the office of *The Crisis* magazine, not some playground!"

"We were just talking about jazz," Aussie said, backing off.

Miss Fauset looked at us both carefully. She wasn't buying what Aussie was saying, but she didn't make too big a deal of it. Later on in the afternoon she came over to where I was sitting putting flyers in envelopes and tried to smooth things over with me. She said she had some jazz records.

A lot of people think they have jazz records when they just have plain old big band music, but I asked her about it. She said that she had been given some records by Mr. Carl Van Vechten and she would try to bring them in.

"And I would appreciate it if you did not get into any more pushing matches with Aussie," she said.

"Hey, I didn't start it," I said.

"Mark, everybody in the world, especially people in our race, looks ahead to figure out how they're going to be doing," Miss Fauset said. "If they don't see too much ahead for themselves they sometimes develop a negative attitude."

"So that's why he acts stupid?"

"That's why sometimes he's a bit difficult," Miss Fauset said.

I liked that *a bit difficult* part and figured I would use it sometimes myself.

If there was anything really stinky to do on the job, either me or Aussie got to do it. Miss Fauset told me to take some drawings up to 67th Street. The address was on the envelope and I was sitting on the uptown train before I noticed that I was going to see Miguel Covarrubias, the Mexican artist who had done a cover for the magazine. On the way up I was wondering if it was going to rain, and not thinking about why I was bringing the drawings uptown. I found the place, and he asked me in. Then he asked me if I would tell him the real reason they were rejecting his drawings.

"I tried really hard to make them nice," he said.

I was going to tell him that I didn't know the real reason or even that they were going to reject them but he got all sad and teary-eyed. I felt really sorry for him. People shouldn't have to feel bad like that. And more than that, I had never seen a grown man cry before.

When I got back to *The Crisis* I told Miss Fauset what had happened and she said that Miguel was a great young artist but was very sensitive.

"That means he cries a lot, right?"

"No, it means that his work represents who he is. And

when his work is turned down he feels that he's being turned down," Miss Fauset said. "We encourage artists to put themselves into their work, but it's risky."

I went back to stapling some dummy magazines and started thinking about Miguel. I also thought about how I would feel if somebody heard me playing my horn and didn't like it. I couldn't see myself crying. No way. I could see me getting a bit difficult, though.

The Fourth of July brought the sound of firecrackers all over the place and when I heard them I thought of gunshots. When Mama left to go to some good-doing meeting about Negroes for the American Flag, I put on the ball game and me and Daddy listened to the Yankees playing a doubleheader. I couldn't figure out why they weren't doing better. Probably because Ruth was in a slump. He'd hit forty-six homers last year. This year he was sleeping.

Me, Henry, and Randy went to the Bronx to see some Negro teams play. The Lincoln Giants, the best Negro League team in New York, played a doubleheader. In the first game, against Portchester, they got three runs in the bottom of the first inning and I knew the game was over. Pryor got four hits and played second base like he owned it. A lot of people say that Hudspeth, playing first base, was the team's best hitter, but I didn't think so. I thought that Pryor could play in the white leagues as well as the Negro leagues.

Then Randy said that the Lincoln Giants were going to lose the second game to a team from Wildwood, New Jersey. I told him that was absolutely impossible and would not happen under any circumstances in this century. The final score? Lincoln Giants 22, Wildwood 2!!!!

When I got home, Lavinia was visiting and Matt was playing "I Dream of Jeanie with the Light Brown Hair" on the piano in the parlor. Why was he playing that when his girlfriend wasn't even named Jeanie unless he was trying to show her how square he was? He was also playing from notes, which is so weak. Matt couldn't make that sorry song jump anyway. I would rather play a number 4 reed with a split lip than play some stupid song about dreaming of Jeanie with some stupid brown hair. I couldn't wait until Matt dragged his moldy butt off to college.

If I knew exactly where Dutch Schultz hung out I would have gone for a walk, naturally taking myself in the opposite direction. I didn't know where he hung out so I laid across my bed and just got madder at Matt, which I didn't mind one bit.

The job at *The Crisis* was not that bad because there wasn't much work to do. Mostly New Negroes came in and sat around and acted smart, which was good because it didn't make me tired. Miss Fauset did not bring in the jazz records. Mr. White, who looked like a white man but was supposed to be black, came in and looked over the bills with Mr. Dill. I found out that Mr. White was an official with the NAACP.

I spent all morning putting issues of *The Crisis* in wrappers. Aussie said that in some parts of the South they would not deliver the magazine. I told him they had to because the post office had to deliver the mail in gloom of night and all that kind of stuff. It was the law. I told the same thing to Miss Fauset when she walked over to the corner we used as a mailroom.

"Is it within the law to lynch people?" she asked.

She didn't stop to wait for my answer so I guess she did not want one.

Everybody at *The Crisis* was scared of Dr. DuBois. When he came into the office everybody sat up straight and tried to look busy. Anytime somebody made a typing error or some other mistake in a letter he just came over to their desk and dropped the letter and walked away. What he was trying to do, Miss Fauset said, was to keep us operating on a high level while we kept the issues of the Negro in front of the American public. I asked Aussie how *The Crisis* was keeping the issues in front of the public if you had to sneak the magazine to people. He told me to ask Dr. DuBois.

Just before lunch Miss Fauset gave me a dollar and told me to go out and buy a corned beef sandwich for Dr.

DuBois and one for his guest, and to make sure that the pickles were fresh.

I went down to the delicatessen just off of Union Square and got the sandwiches and told the guy behind the counter to make sure the pickles were fresh and he told me to pick out my own, which I did.

The guest was Countee Cullen, who Miss Fauset had mentioned as being one of the best young poets. He had dark, shiny eyes that kept darting around as if he was expecting something scary to happen. Miss Fauset said he was twenty-two, but he looked a lot younger. He could have been my age. He had just published a book of poems. Miss Fauset liked that kind of thing but I didn't see anything to sitting around reading poetry.

"He's a brilliant young man," she said. The way she said it made me think she was talking about a chocolate éclair or something else good to eat. "You'd be smart to remember his name."

I was glad my name wasn't Countee.

When I returned from the delicatessen Mr. Countee was sitting in Dr. DuBois's office with his new book. It had the title, *Color*, on the cover. Dr. DuBois was looking over the book and smiling to beat the band. Miss Fauset brought me in and Countee stood up and shook my hand, which made me feel good. Miss Fauset asked Countee, as she called him, if he wanted to go to a party. He said he would try to make it and she gave him the address.

Later, Miss Fauset said that when they spoke of the New Negro it was exactly people like Countee Cullen they were speaking about. I had finally figured out just what she was talking about when she referred to the New Negro. It helped if you looked a little square and spoke like you were trying to taste the words as they were coming out, but mostly you had to be doing stuff that Old Negroes weren't doing.

She asked me if I wrote poetry or stories. I said no, but I thought I could write music someday. Then she asked me if I wanted to go to the party to which she had invited Countee Cullen. I said okay. She wrote down the address and the person's name who was giving the party and told me that if anyone asked who had sent me just to say that I was from *The Crisis*. She told me not to forget my tie. I knew that.

At exactly fifteen minutes past three I got yelled at by Miss Effie Lee Newsome and everybody else in the office. Miss Newsome wrote the children's page in *The Crisis* and was only there part-time. She came in with some photographs and poems and went over them with Miss Fauset. Then Dr. DuBois came out of his office and greeted her. Everybody called her "Effie." When she went to speak to Mr. Dill, the business manager, I read some of the poems.

They were all right, but I thought I could have written some of them. When she came away from Mr. Dill and was ready to leave I thought she had forgotten the poems and took them to her. I said, "Oh, Effie, you forgot the poems."

I got it from Miss Newsome and Miss Fauset. Who was I to call Miss Newsome by her first name? Who did I think I was? I was apologizing all over the place. Miss Newsome looked as if her head was going to explode or something. It was absolutely gruesome.

"Don't you dare disrespect someone like Miss Newsome!" Miss Fauset said. "Who do you think you are?"

I had learned enough at *The Crisis* not to answer that question.

When I got home I told Mama about being invited to the party and she asked me if it was a decent party or one of those loud, low-life parties. I told her Miss Fauset and Countee Cullen were going to be there and maybe even Dr. DuBois, so I knew it was not going to be low-life. She asked me who they were and I said they were New Negroes. Then Daddy asked me if they were working and I said yes, and he said they couldn't be that bad.

Mama wanted me to go to Friday night church services at Abyssinian Baptist with her. I didn't want to go but I didn't want to hear her mouth, either. When we got to the church there was the usual crowd and a few kids my age who had got trapped. Adam Clayton Powell, Sr., preached the sermon. He was talking about how hard Job had it. First Job got this problem, then he got that problem, then he got another problem. By the time Job got around to having his fifth or sixth problem, I was falling asleep.

When the services were finally over, Mrs. Lucas, who knew more gossip than the *Amsterdam News,* said that Reverend Powell's son, Adam, Jr., was getting ready to go to Colgate College. Adam, the Junior version, was so light-skinned I thought he had to be a New Negro or at least kind of New. Sister Givens, whose daughter, Elizabeth, was the sweetest child this side of Paradise, said that Adam, Jr., was smart, but that he was a little fast for a minister's son.

Edie Waller, Fats's sister, is good people. But she is like Fats in that she is big in every part she has. She has big feet, big legs, big hips, a big body, and even a big head. She has a nice smile, but it's still coming out that big head of hers.

Elizabeth Givens is little and stuck on herself but she's so cute you pretend you don't see it. If she and Edie were walking past a mirror she would be the one to stop, check herself out, and maybe even throw herself a kiss.

After services I found Elizabeth and asked her if she wanted to walk across 125th Street with me. She said she did not, but asked me if I wanted to come to a tea next Saturday at her house. A singer from Philadelphia named Marian Anderson was going to sing. I told Elizabeth, knowing her mother was the kind of woman who liked to put on airs, I hoped she wasn't going to sing opera.

Elizabeth said she probably would sing opera. Stupid me said that I did not want to come. Then Elizabeth said she would ask Robert Gause. That was supposed to hurt me because Robert Gause put it out that he was all blue vein and top shelf. But to me he was just working his holier-than-thou attitude and pretending his people came over on the *Mayflower* and settled right on Sugar Hill.

I told Elizabeth I would see her when I saw her and she said that whenever she saw me it would be too soon. Oh, well. It wasn't my fault that Elizabeth did not recognize quality when she saw it.

■ ■ ■ ■ ■ ■ ■ ■ ■ ■ ■ ■ ■ ■ ■ ■ ■ ■ ■

SOME MYSTERIOUS STRANGERS COME AROUND; I HAVE A SERIOUS TALK WITH FATS WALLER, IN THE MIDDLE OF WHICH I GET A BRILLIANT IDEA AND A BAD SCARE.

■ ■ ■ ■ ■ ■ ■ ■ ■ ■ ■ ■ ■ ■ ■ ■ ■ ■ ■

Mama came in the house singing "There Is a Balm in Gilead." Daddy asked what she was so happy about and she said she was happy because all her bills were paid.

"There's two bill collectors downstairs looking at the mailboxes," Mama said. "Least I guess they're bill collectors 'cause they're white and mean-looking. But all my bills are paid. My finances, except for Matt's college, are so good they're almost sanctified!"

"Those bill collectors could be hoodlums," I said, thinking about a certain Dutch Schultz.

"Ain't no hoodlums." Daddy sniffed hard the way he does sometimes. "Ain't no white hoodlums going to come all the way uptown to Harlem to get our little bit of cash."

I hoped they weren't coming for anybody's fingers, either. Not that I was scared or anything. But I did think maybe it would be a smooth idea not to go out until the next day.

In the morning I wore a white shirt and carried my jacket over my arm. I had been wearing the jacket the night we picked up Schultz's booze and I didn't want to be seen in it again.

Mr. Dill made out the checks for the May issue. Langston Hughes got two dollars for a poem that had only twenty-five words, counting the title. That was eight cents a word! The writing business was starting to look better.

Miss Fauset went around the office trying to get everybody to sign a letter to Mayor Hylan saying that Samuel Battle, the highest-ranking Negro cop on the New York police force, should not have been passed over for promotion. She got everybody to sign it, including me, but Dr. DuBois wouldn't even look at it. He said when people are being lynched you don't worry about litter on the way to the lynching tree. I thought Miss Fauset was going to cry, but she didn't. I thought Dr. DuBois was probably very smart and everything, but he could also be kind of cold.

Miss Fauset said she was going shopping over to Klein's department store on her lunch break, and I said I would go with her.

"Mark, that's very nice of you," she said.

That made me feel good but it was embarrassing when she took my arm.

Klein's was one nice store with twice as much stuff as Blumstein's on 125th Street. I saw some black people shopping there but none working there, as usual. Miss Fauset bought two blue towels, two blue washcloths, and a little glass elephant. She asked me if I liked the elephant.

"No."

She said it would have been polite to say that I liked it.

When we got back to *The Crisis* office, there was a small group of people sitting around listening to Dr. DuBois. Margaret J. Washington had died, and Dr. DuBois was talking about her husband, Booker T.

"Booker T. was a man who meant well, but could not see farther than the end of his nose," Dr. DuBois said. "He was so busy pleasing white folks and got so good at it that he thought that was the only thing for the Negro to do. I wish I could have sat him down and talked with him man-to-man for an evening. The fact that I didn't was more my fault than his."

Dr. DuBois had given me a good idea. Henry and I had already decided that we needed to get Fats on the job to get the money we owed to Dutch Schultz. The truth was that Fats wasn't an easy person to talk to. He was always smiling and rolling his eyes and looking like he was really laughing at everything he saw. But he was also big so I didn't want to jump up into his face or do anything too spiky. That's when I thought of inviting him to the party that Miss Fauset had invited me to. Then we could sit around with the swells and I would sort of ask him how he was going to help us get the money we needed. The more I thought about it the more I knew it was one of the best ideas I had ever had.

Dr. DuBois had sounded annoyed when he was talking about Booker T. Washington but he was always sounding annoyed about something so I didn't pay it that much mind. Just as he was getting into the second part of his being mad, the part where he would stop every now and then and nod his head, the door to the office flew open and this lady kind of flew in.

"Good afternoon, Miss Walker!" Miss Fauset said, smiling all over the place.

I knew that A'Lelia Walker was the one who had the ads for Madam C. J. Walker products on the back cover of *The Crisis*. She was wearing a shiny pink dress and strings of pearls that came down all the way to her hips and swung around when she walked. She had two huge shopping bags with her. When she finished writing out a check for her company's ads, she asked Miss Fauset if somebody could help her with her packages. Miss Fauset volunteered me and I had to carry the packages to the elevator, and then out to her car.

The car was a huge Packard and it was sharp! I put the two shopping bags in the back and Miss Walker got into the front seat.

"You're such a dear boy," she said. "Are you an author?"

"No, ma'am," I said.

She didn't answer but gave me a quick little smile that probably meant the same thing as *plebeian*.

I watched as she started the car and she winked at me before pulling out into traffic. If I could ever afford a car like that I would be in heaven.

When I got back to the office, Miss Fauset told me to sit down next to her. Then she asked me if I knew why Dr. DuBois had problems with Booker T. Washington. Miss Fauset had a way of sitting down and looking you right in the face, like a teacher. If you weren't sure of yourself, she was going to find you out.

"He always has a problem with somebody," I said. "But Booker T. Washington's dead so I don't see why . . ."

Wrong answer. Miss Fauset looked at me like I was something pitiful, shook her head, and walked into the corner that doubled as her office. It didn't make any sense to me. If I knew all the right answers before she asked them, then there wasn't any reason for her to ask them in the first place. And if she wanted to ask the questions, then she should be glad that I didn't know the answers. Still, I was getting to like Miss Fauset. A lot. She had a way of making me feel stupid on the outside and warm on the inside at the same time. I think it had something to do with her being a New Woman.

On the way home I stopped off at the theater and waited around until the movie was over. Fats was sitting at the theater's organ.

"Hey, Fats."

"Hey, Groovy, you're in the movie," Fats said.

"Look, you want to come to a party downtown tomorrow night?" I asked. "It's mostly white folks but it'll probably be all right."

"White folks is good if they're the right folks," Fats said, taking the address I handed him. "It's free to get in?"

"Yeah."

"Don't you like that about white people?"

"I guess," I said. "I thought at the party we could talk about the truck and the booze and stuff."

"Do me a favor, will you?" Fats leaned his big head close to mine. "Go tell that dude sitting on the end in the second row that somebody wants to see him in the back."

I turned and looked in the direction that Fats had nodded his head. There was one man sitting in the second row, right on the aisle. I felt Fats give me a little nudge and I felt just a little bit afraid. Fats nudged me again and I stood and walked over to the man.

"I think there's somebody that wants to see you in the back," I said.

The man grabbed me by the collar and pulled me close

so I could smell the garlic on his breath. "Is that Thomas W. Waller over there on the organ?" he asked.

I sort of turned the best I could with the guy holding my shirt but Fats was gone. When the guy stood he was at least fifteen, maybe forty feet tall, and his big hand felt like a clamp around my neck. He marched me up the aisle and out into the lobby of the theater.

"You tell your friend that if he doesn't show up in court next week about his child support payments, I'm going to personally remove some parts from his body to make sure he doesn't have any more children. You understand that?"

I really couldn't talk with his knee pressing into my groin, but I did a lot of nodding.

On the way home I stopped off at Henry's and told him what happened.

"Yeah, Fats was married when he was sixteen and had a kid and everything," Henry said. "Most of his life is over. That's why he don't care about nothing."

"I wonder why everybody says they're going to take something off his body?"

"'Cause he's so big they probably figure he won't miss it," Henry said. "They probably think they're doing him a favor. I heard they trail him all around waiting to see him get some money. I'm not going to hang around him anymore. Wherever he is, Henry ain't gonna be!"

"Ain't gonna be *what*?" I asked.

"Ain't gonna be around him!" Henry said.

"Okay, that sounds hip," I said. "But if we don't get that booze back or the money to pay for it we 'ain't gonna be' *breathing!*"

"So what are you going to do?"

"I'm going to this party downtown," I said. "And I told Fats to come."

"Anybody ever tell you how dumb you are?" Henry asked.

"Look, Henry, Fats is at where we want to be," I said. "We have to stay on his good side. If he likes us we can be making a record in no time."

"Or be in big trouble," Henry said. "And if we don't get some practice in we're not going to make a record, anyway."

"Did I tell you I got the whole 'Sugar Foot Stomp' memorized?" I asked him. "I can really swing it, man."

The look on Henry's face was mainly surprise, but I could see he was also admiring me because the "Sugar Foot Stomp" was really hot.

"You are really okay," Henry said, patting me on the shoulder. "I think you're going to be the jazz man of the future."

I didn't exactly have the piece down but I had played along with the record a few times. I didn't want to tell that to Henry because I didn't want to mess up how good he was feeling about me.

I GO TO MR. KNOPF'S PARTY AND FEEL WONDERFUL AND SMART AND SAY SOME REALLY INTERESTING THINGS TO PEOPLE, BUT THEN IT IS ALL SPOILED WHEN FATS MEETS THE FAT LADY.

Mr. Alfred Knopf's house wasn't far from the Plaza Hotel. When I arrived at the party there were at least thirty people there, and at least seven or eight Negroes. Most of the time people just stood around, holding drinks in their hands and talking. Two waiters kept going around with drinks or little sandwiches on a tray. I didn't see anybody paying for the sandwiches so when the waiter offered them to me I took two. What I took was the little frankfurters that had been baked in a little frankfurter roll. They were all right, but nothing special.

"You look very neat tonight," Miss Fauset said.

"You look very neat also," I said. She had on a dress the same light brown color as her skin but the dress was shiny and with all the lights in Mr. Knopf's house it almost looked as if Miss Fauset was moving when she was standing still. I was thinking she was looking foxy but I got my mind off that real quick.

Miss Fauset seemed to know everybody at the party and I didn't know anybody so I wandered over to the wall and just looked around. A woman in a maid's outfit asked me if I cared for champagne, but before I could answer her she said she would bring me a lemonade. It took her a minute to bring the lemonade, but it was in the kind of glass you drink champagne out of, so it made me feel good.

As soon as Countee Cullen came in, Mr. Knopf took him by the arm and led him to a small group of white people who gathered around him. Langston Hughes arrived a little later and somebody else grabbed him and started talking to him. It looked like the Negroes at the party were the stars. I wasn't a star and didn't even know what to do or where to stand. Miss Fauset came over once and told me to mingle, but I didn't even know how to do that. I felt a little stupid just standing in the middle of the room holding the lemonade but when I looked around I saw a lot of people doing the same thing.

After a while Langston Hughes saw me and came over and asked me if I felt uncomfortable. I said yes and he said he did, too.

"But I've figured out that's the way you're supposed to feel at a cocktail party. The ones who really have this thing down the best are the ones in the tuxedos," he said, smiling a little crooked grin. "They can manage to look good standing in the middle of a room doing nothing. That's talent. You'll catch on after a while."

"I guess that's what I have to learn to do, Mr. Hughes," I said.

"Call me Langston," he said, laughing. "Look, you want to go to a real party this week? Thursday night and the live-ins are stepping out. Good music, good food, and three kinds of sweat."

"Yeah, sure," I answered. I felt good and a little jumpy having Langston Hughes talk to me.

"I'll drop the address off at *The Crisis* office," he said. "Now we have to work on standing around and smiling as if we know something."

"Langston! Langston!" Another white woman was waving to him.

"My godmother," he said, and then he slid through the crowd to where she was standing.

It was interesting that he should have a white godmother.

I liked Langston. He smiled a lot when he talked and made everything sound like a joke but he seemed like a real person. The funny thing was that he was supposed to be a New Negro and was being published all over the place but he seemed very ordinary when he was just standing around, as if he was comfortable being whoever he was. He had a way of making me feel comfortable, too, and that made the party easier. Countee Cullen never seemed completely comfortable. He kept shifting his weight from one foot to the other and he never moved his elbows away from his side.

The party didn't really seem like it was happening at the same time I was there. I mean, I was there, but the people were kind of gliding around the room as if they were in a movie. The women all had the same kind of way of not really laughing but making a noise like they were announcing something funny. After a while I was catching on, like Langston said I would.

I had noticed a black woman, really tall, and skinny in the soft kind of way that some tall women have. She was sitting at one of the small tables near the wall. When an older white man whispered something in her ear she smiled. It was a nice smile and right then and there I liked her, too. She said something to the man who had whispered to her, stood up, and walked over to the piano. I had seen pictures of her before and finally realized who she was, Ethel Waters.

The piano player wore a tuxedo and Miss Waters said something to him and he nodded back. He started playing and, after a while, the talking quieted down. Then Miss Waters started singing and she could really sing. It was a sweet song called "There'll Be Some Changes Made." I had heard the song played faster but I could still imagine myself playing as she sang, my saxophone sounding all growly and bluesy, and she turning to me with that big smile of hers and those big eyes. When Miss Waters finished, everyone applauded. Some people shouted out for an encore but Miss Waters just smiled and sat down.

"And so . . . what do you think of the Scopes trial?" a man asked me. He had silver-white hair but only around the edges of his head. The middle part was bald and shiny.

"I don't know," I said.

"Well, it's not as important a trial as everyone is pretending," he said. "You can believe that. The truth of the matter is that the New York papers are playing it up as if it threatens modern knowledge, but I only believe that it shows the ignorance of the people of Tennessee. Evolution is here to stay. You can't argue with science. It's just not possible."

I remembered something about the trial from school, that it was about a teacher breaking the law by teaching something that was against the Bible.

"Some things in science change," I said.

He leaned very close to me. "Not evolution, my friend, not evolution. We are descended from monkeys. My great-great-great-great-whatever-grandfather probably swung from a tree and was glad of it! The people in Tennessee are just ignorant!"

"If you're rich you don't mind being called a monkey," I said. "I think the people in Tennessee aren't that rich."

"Now that's insightful. That's very, very insightful. You're a writer? Perhaps a poet?"

"A poet," I said.

He kept on talking while I wondered why I had said I was a poet. Maybe it was the party with everybody standing around not really doing anything and still being swell and all. Like Langston said, they were good at it, too. Someone called the man I was talking to and beckoned for him to come over to where they were sitting. He took me by the arm and I started to go with him when I saw Fats walk into the room. One of the butlers was with him. Fats was dressed in a black suit and had a derby perched on the side of his head looking as if it might fall off any minute. He looked around, saw me, and pointed with one of his fat fingers. The butler nodded and stepped away from him.

I could see Fats was a little tipsy as he made his way over to me.

"He actually asked me did I have an invitashun!" Fats said. "Can you imagine that?"

"Have you been . . . ?" I didn't even finish the question. Fats reeked of booze. Through the crowd I saw Miss Fauset easing toward me.

"So tell me, Mark, how are you tonight?" Fats asked. "And when you woke up this morning what did you find in your mind beside your name and your fame?"

"Fats, you got to be cool," I whispered. "I wanted you

to come to the party to meet some swell white folks so we can try to get the money — oh, hello, Miss Fauset."

"Mark, is this a friend of yours?" she asked. Her voice came out so sideways it almost cut me.

"Yes, ma'am."

"And you invited him to this party?"

"No, ma'am," Fats said in this real loud voice. "He hired me to play the piano for the good white folks!"

Fats had spied the baby grand and went over to it and sat down.

"I think you had better get him out of here!" Miss Fauset was hissing at me.

Fats hit a loud chord and everybody stopped and turned around.

"Don't worry about it, folks," he said. "That's just my unevolved hand monkeying around."

A few people laughed at that but a few looked a little nervous when Fats slammed his hand down on the piano again. He giggled a little and Miss Fauset looked as if she was going to faint.

"Can we all say a little prayer for that hand?" Fats asked. "Maybe if we combine prayer and evolution something good will happen." Fats turned, looked at his left hand, which was now on the piano bench, and we all watched as he made it climb up the side of the piano toward the keyboard.

"Mark, do something!" Miss Fauset's face was scrunched up around her nose.

While Fats's left hand was climbing up the side of the piano he was making the sign of the cross with his right hand and praying. Then his left hand got up to the keyboard and it, or he, started playing classical music and everybody in the room started clapping. Fats looked as if he was the most surprised of all of us and his eyes got wide and started rolling around his head and people started clapping again. Then his right hand started climbing up his leg and jumped onto the piano. But his right hand started playing jazz and that's when Ethel Waters stood up and clapped and then it was all over.

Fats played for twenty minutes straight, stopping only to put both hands together and saying, "Somebody get me a drink!"

Well, he was the big hit and everybody loved him until a fat woman asked him if he could write songs. She wanted a song for her grandson's birthday.

"And I understand that Negroes are so inventive!" she said.

Fats rolled his eyes up and said he could write a song if she needed one.

"I could write a song about you," he said, leaning over the edge of the piano bench. "Turn around so I can see you good."

She turned around. I looked at Miss Fauset. She was smiling. Fats started singing.

> *"All that meat in your caboose*
> *I just hope it don't come loose*
> *'Cause if it did I'd surely have to run*
> *Oh, that meat is wide and wavy*
> *All it needs is a little gravy*
> *But if it comes at me, I'll surely have to run. . . ."*

The lady looked a little embarrassed at first, but she laughed when everybody else started laughing and gave Fats a look as if they were old friends or something.

Me and Fats were at the party for another half hour and when we left, most of the people clapped. I guessed if you could play as good as Fats it didn't much matter what else you did. Miss Fauset said she would see me bright and early Monday morning. This time she was talking with her teeth clenched tight. She really looked tough. I liked that.

When I got home Mama was waiting for me. She asked me if I knew what time it was. Then, before I could answer she told me that it was almost midnight. Then she told me that she had never been so disappointed in her whole life. Then she told me that one day I would be sitting home waiting for my child to come home and then I would know how she felt.

I MEET MR. WALLACE THURMAN AND DECIDE THAT BEING STRANGE IS ALL RIGHT IF YOU ARE STRANGE IN AN INTERESTING WAY.

If you ever embarrass me again the way you did the other night I will take off my shoe and beat you in your head until your ears bleed!" Miss Fauset's eyes were squinched up and the cup of water she held in her hand was shaking.

"Yes, ma'am."

"Who was that clown?"

"His name is Fats Waller," I said.

"Fats? *Fats?* What kind of a name is Fats? And did you know he was drunk when he came in the door? And do you know who he was insulting with his little song? Only the wife of one of the NAACP's biggest contributors!"

"Yes, ma'am."

"And do you have his address?"

"I'll tell him not to show up at any more parties," I said.

"Mr. Van Vechten, for whatever odd reason, wants to

get in contact with him," Miss Fauset said. "Write down his name and address and give it to me by the end of the day. Otherwise, please refrain from speaking to me as much as possible."

"Yes, ma'am."

At the party Langston said I would learn how to stand around and be uncomfortable like everybody else. At the office I was learning how not to decide what was going on until somebody told me. Miss Fauset said she hated Fats, but she still wanted his address to give to somebody.

Fats didn't have a regular place, but was staying with a family downtown around St. Nicholas Park. He said they had a telephone but I had forgotten the name of the family so I couldn't get his number and address from the telephone book.

I was thinking more and more about being a writer. It looked like a pretty easy way of making a living. The thing was, Langston Hughes and Countee Cullen were not that much older than me. I didn't know how much money they got for writing a book, but at eight cents a word, which is what I knew Langston got paid for one of his poems, I'd be home writing all day! I figured out that I needed to write 12,500 words at eight cents each to make a thousand dollars. If I was a full-time writer I could write 500 words every day for $40, which would put me square in the

Pullman car of the gravy train. Then at night I could go out and play with my band.

No wonder people liked writing. I knew I needed to learn more about it, so at lunchtime I walked over to Fourth Avenue and looked in some of the used bookstores. One of the owners asked me what I was looking for and I told him something interesting. He gave me a copy of *Moby Dick* for ten cents and said if I didn't like it I could bring it back.

"What's it about?" I asked.

"It's about a man's struggle to kill a ferocious whale," he said. "But it's a symbol for all of man's struggles against the world and against himself."

"Why did he want to kill it?"

"Well, it bit his leg off, but that's not the important part," the bookstore guy said. "The important part is the underlying story about man's finding himself in the world."

I knew that if a whale bit my leg off I would want to kill him, too. That's what I was thinking about when I started back to the office, but then I remembered that I wanted to see what was playing at the movie house on Third Avenue and 11th Street, so I walked down there. Then I saw that I was going to be late getting back from lunch and ran all the way back to *The Crisis* office. It was pretty hot and I was sweaty when I got back. Mr. Dill made a comment about me investing in a bar of soap. He did not have to say that.

Miss Fauset (who had heard Mr. Dill) said something about how everyone who worked at *The Crisis* was also working for the NAACP and was representing the entire Negro race and how we had to make sure we were clean and nicely dressed. I knew she was already mad at me so it didn't make any difference if she got madder.

One of the things I liked about working at *The Crisis* was the strange people who showed up there. I was used to seeing strange people in the neighborhood but they were usually just crazy, or shell-shocked from the war or just a little bit strange in the way they dressed or moved. But at *The Crisis* they were strange and a poet, or strange *and* a politician, or even strange *and* important, which went together sometimes. So when the door opened and a little black fellow came in with an armful of papers and announced himself I just sat back to catch the show.

"Wallace Thurman has arrived!" he called out.

One of the typists glanced up but she ignored him and went back to her work.

"As Noah was before the flood so is Wallace before the fire!" he went on.

"How are you doing, Mr. Thurman?" Miss Fauset said. She was holding herself kind of stiff.

"I am here to announce the premature death of the New Negro and the rise of the Old Colored folks," was the answer.

Mr. Thurman brought the papers he was carrying to an empty desk and dropped them in a heap. He was a little fellow, black as the ace of spades, with a funny little grin on his face as if he didn't take himself too seriously. I liked that. He stood in the middle of the floor, the brim of his hat just over his eyes, and went on about how the New Negro didn't mean much to him and how he thought it was all being faked for the white press.

"But I am going to tell the truth," he said.

"And publish it where?" Miss Fauset asked. "Are you still working on your magazine?"

"*Fire*, the magazine for young black voices, will be off press soon and will destroy the illusion of newness that you are pushing onto the people."

"Yes, Wallace," Miss Fauset said. "And what can we do for you today?"

"The National Association for the Advancement of Colored People can advance me two dollars so I can take my Colored self up to Harlem," Wallace said. "Not that I am without funds. I have here a check for one hundred dollars, but, as you see, it is a check and therefore not negotiable in our subway system."

"Did you sell a book?" Mr. Dill asked.

"I am writing a history of life in Harlem," Wallace said. "It will be in the *Haldeman-Julius Quarterly*."

Mr. Dill gave Wallace the $2.00 and talked to him while Miss Fauset looked over some of the papers he had dropped on the desk.

When Wallace left I asked Miss Fauset why she didn't like him.

"Didn't I tell you this morning not to speak to me?" Miss Fauset asked.

"Yes, ma'am."

"Thurman Wallace is a very talented, very bright young man who hasn't found himself," Miss Fauset said. "He is looking around at life in Harlem and only seeing the surface. He sees people standing around in the streets with nothing to do, or working at laboring jobs and he thinks that he's seen the limits of Negro life. What he does not see is the talented tenth that will lead our people into exciting new areas and make the accomplishments that will establish our place in American society. I also know that he doesn't realize that he is part of that talented tenth."

"The talented tenth? Who are they?"

"I'll point them out to you when they come into the office," Miss Fauset said.

"How come he doesn't know it?" I asked.

"It takes some people longer than others to find

themselves," she said. "And you can just hope they find themselves before they ruin their lives. I don't expect you to understand that, Mark."

That was a good point about me not understanding it, because I didn't. I knew that Miss Fauset was getting comfortable with me, though. She was enjoying getting on my case. She talked to me a lot more than she did to Aussie. I knew I was a lot better-looking than Aussie and a lot smarter, but it was more than that.

What I was beginning to catch on to was that there were a lot of people who lived in an ordinary way and did okay with their lives. Then there were people who were always trying to do something great, and they were probably the New Negro crowd. I thought that it probably didn't matter what you looked like so much as what you were going to do with your life, and Miss Fauset was trying to figure out if I was a New Negro or just an ordinary Negro. I was wondering about that myself.

I got home and Mama was mad because Daddy had hit the numbers. He had hit 0-6-5, which was his number because he was born on June 5. He got $27 for a nickel straight bet but Mama was mad because he was gambling.

"Do you think the good Lord wants gamblers in His heaven?" Mama asked.

"Ginny, I don't know what the Lord wants and what He don't want," Daddy said. "I wasn't gambling, anyway. I just put a nickel down on 0-6-5 because Boo-Boo — you know long-headed Boo-Boo from 138th Street?"

"I know that low-lifed man!"

"Well, he said I looked lucky and I was just trying to figure out if he was right or not."

Wrong answer. Mama started boo-hooing and said that she was going to have to tithe the $27 but she was still ashamed to face the Lord. Daddy said that the Lord asked for ten percent and not to be pushing Him to take more. Mama got in a huff, took the three dollars Daddy pushed toward her, and went out to Monday night prayer meeting. Least she didn't ask us to go with her.

Me and Daddy went to a basketball game at the 135th Street YMCA. The Harlem Rens were going to play two games, the first against the Morningside Comanches and the second against the Jersey City Whirlwinds.

The Rens were a great team, maybe the best team in the United States. They beat the Comanches easy, but the Comanches were just a team run by the Elks. The game against Jersey City was supposed to be the tough game. It wasn't.

The game was close for about two minutes, and then the Rens ran away with it. When we got home I asked Daddy if he thought the white professional teams would ever play against the Negro teams.

"If I was a white man and had a basketball team I

wouldn't let them play against no Negro team," Daddy said. He had taken off his socks and was cutting his toenails in the kitchen like he wasn't even worried that Mama was going to stick her key in the door and catch him. "Because if a bunch of smokies beat my all-white team, people are going to start looking at each other and asking what else can a Negro do better than a white man? And the thing is, it's better keeping the races apart so that you can't make the comparison. That way you can definitely say you're the best."

"You think the Negroes would win?"

"I know they would."

"Isn't that just racial prejudice the same as some white people got?" I asked.

"Sure it is," Daddy said. "But it's coming from me, so I don't mind a bit."

Later Daddy had to go to work. Since the Cotton Club was closed down for a few weeks, he had got a job cleaning off tables at Small's. I asked if I could go with him and he said I might as well because Mama was mad already so it didn't make a lot of difference.

THINGS ARE LOOKING UP UNTIL WE FIND A DEAD WATERMELON AT THE END OF THE RAINBOW.

Friday and I was off from work but Mama was shaking me and saying that my friend Randy was in the kitchen all excited about something. I sat up and tried to get my head together when Randy burst into the room.

"You read the paper yesterday?" he asked, sticking an *Amsterdam News* two inches in front of my nose.

"Naw, why don't you just tell me who got killed," I said.

"Nobody got killed," Randy said. "I mean, somebody must have got killed but that's not why I'm here. Here, read this piece."

BLACK SWAN AUDITIONS

HARRY PACE, NOTED RECORD PRODUCER AND OWNER OF BLACK SWAN RECORDS, ANNOUNCES AUDITIONS FOR MUSICIANS THIS COMING FRIDAY EVENING AT THE RENAISSANCE CASINO AND BALLROOM. WINNERS WILL GET RECORDING CONTRACTS WITH THE FAMED HARLEM LABEL. "I AM INTERESTED IN NEW YOUNG TALENT," SAID THE OWNER OF THIS DYNAMIC COMPANY. AUDITIONS BEGIN AT 7 P.M.

"New young talent," Randy said. "That's us. We get to the Renaissance Casino and Ballroom, we play like champs, blow everybody away, and get a big record contract!"

"You think we can do it?"

"Sure we can. I told Henry and he's coming over in a few minutes. He's picking up the sheet music for 'Sweet Georgia Brown' from his cousin."

"Sweet Georgia Brown" wasn't the most swingingest piece around but we played it well and we mostly knew it by heart. I got up and started dressing while Randy added up how much money we would make on our first record deal.

"I heard you get seven cents a record," he said.

"That's all?"

"That's enough if they sell as many records as Trixie Smith or Ethel Waters," Randy said. "Ethel Waters sold three hundred thousand records last year. That's about . . . a lot of money apiece. We're going to have so much money we won't know what to do with it. We're going to have to get secretaries and things just to keep our business straight."

We went into the kitchen and Mama was making breakfast and yelling at Daddy for sitting at the kitchen table in his underwear.

"Randy's seen underwear before," Daddy said.

"Not in my kitchen he hasn't," Mama said. "Go put some clothes on, Benny."

Daddy got up, took another sip of his coffee, and went into the bedroom.

"We're going to have to practice all day, Mama," I said. "They're having auditions at the Renaissance Casino and Ballroom tonight."

"Why do they have to have that jazz music in nightclubs and bars if it's supposed to be so good?" Mama asked. "You never hear nobody playing any of that music in church and I know why."

"Why?" Randy asked.

"Because the Lord don't like jazz," Mama said.

Even Randy was smart enough to leave that alone.

Henry got to the house with the sheet music. The music was all in G, which was good because it was an easy key to play in.

"I got an idea for an arrangement," Randy said. "We start off with just the sax playing the melody line. Then the guitar comes in with a few chords, then there's a thing back and forth between the guitar and the sax. Make it like you're talking to each other. You know what I mean?"

"What are we talking about?" Henry asked.

"You're not talking about anything," Randy said. "It's *as if* you're talking to each other."

"I got it," I said. "Let's give it a try. Henry'll get it."

I was really anxious to get going because I knew that if we hit a record contract with Black Swan we'd have it made in the shade. I dropped a couple of reeds into a glass of water while I finished off some scrambled eggs and toast and listened to more of what Henry had to say about the arrangement. I was going to start, then me and Henry were going to play, then we would really pick up the beat when Randy came in on the ivories. At the end, Randy would kind of fade out and me and Henry would go back and forth again, and then I would end the piece. It was smoking.

"You ought to surprise everybody and play gospel," Mama said. "You know Black Swan has some gospel recordings."

Henry gave me a look but he didn't say anything because we didn't talk about our mamas.

We went to the living room to practice and Daddy came in, dressed in his pants and an old shirt, and sat down to listen.

I started in on the first licks and it was sounding good already. Mama came in and started talking, right in the middle of my solo.

"Mama, I'm trying to practice," I said.

"Not only can't the Lord have one of His songs played in this house but I can't even talk in my own living room."

"You can talk, Mrs. Purvis," Randy piped up. "We just want to do good when we audition this evening."

"I'm sure you'll do all right if you trust in the Lord," Mama said.

Mama gave Randy a smile, Henry another smile, and me a stern look that made me smile.

We played the song a few more times and Henry was liking it but I wasn't sure. The bad part was when Randy and I were supposed to be going back and forth. The Randy man just wasn't saying anything. I asked Daddy how we sounded.

"I've heard better and I've heard worse," he said. "You boys are sort of leaning away from the better."

"Thanks for the encouragement," I said.

The Renaissance was on 133rd Street and Seventh

Avenue. They showed movies on the first floor and the second was where all the Big-Time happenings went on. When we walked in I felt a chill go through my body. There were at least a hundred guys there already. Most of them were black but there were some Spanish dudes and even a few white guys with slicked-back hair. Some were running through their riffs, others were just standing around holding their horns. Most of them were wearing suits, too.

"I should have worn my tuxedo," Henry said. He was almost whispering.

"You don't have a tuxedo," I said.

Randy went over to the sign-up desk and put our name on the list.

It was exactly five minutes to seven on the wall clock when the first group started to play. It was a five-piece band with two cornets, a saxophone, piano, and skins. They were just flat-out good. By the time they finished at least fifteen people had left. I got a sinking feeling in my stomach.

"We should have practiced more," Henry said.

I looked around at all the other fellows and how serious they looked and I knew we should have practiced more. All the time I thought the New Negro was just writing poems and being la-de-da and all of a sudden I was seeing some jazz dudes who acted all serious. I was worried but I knew it was time to pinch butt and go for it.

"Jazz is about tunes but it's about improvising, too," I

said. "We'll just have to get into the improvising a little more."

The next two groups were just about as good as the first one and I wondered if we had any chance at all. Henry pointed out that a lot of players were leaving and I knew they were leaving because the competition was just too good. A man I figured was Harry Pace, the owner of Black Swan Records, shook everybody's hand when they finished playing.

It was a quarter to nine when we were called. My legs were weak when we got up to the stand but I was determined not to mess up. That's what I was thinking when I heard Randy start playing. Only he wasn't playing "Sweet Georgia Brown." He was playing the "See See Rider Blues." I looked over at Henry and he was playing along with him. I didn't know what was happening but I played along the best I could even though I didn't know anything but the melody. We played for about three minutes and then, since we didn't know where we were going, just sort of stopped.

I looked around the room and everybody else was just ignoring us, like we weren't even there. The way I was feeling was two steps and a jump past terrible.

Mr. Pace shook our hand and said he'd let us know.

"I thought we were supposed to be playing 'Sweet Georgia Brown'?" I said, as we started down the stairs.

"I froze up and couldn't think of how it started," Randy

said. "I knew we were supposed to be playing it but there was something we were going to do at the beginning, right?"

"Yeah, Mark was supposed to start and me and him were supposed to be talking and stuff, remember?" Henry said. "You blew the whole thing, Randy."

"Look, I'm sorry, guys, but . . ."

"You fellows sounded pretty good," a gruff voice behind us said. "Who you working for now?"

I turned and saw two white guys at the top of the stairs. Both of them were wearing suits and I figured they were businessmen.

"We've been laying a little low trying to put some new ideas together," Henry said.

"Hey, we don't want to steal you away from Black Swan," the taller guy said. "But if you boys want to make some pretty good money this weekend we'd love to have you play at our club."

"Yeah, well, that could happen," Henry said, nudging me with his elbow.

"Why don't you take a ride over to our club, take a look at it, and if you like the setup, we'll book you for this weekend." He had an easy smile but he looked kind of square with his hair parted in the middle. Actually, I thought I had seen him someplace before. Maybe at the Cotton Club. "I'm Jack and this is Tony G. He has a real ear for music."

"Yeah, we got some time to kill," Henry said.

"Sure thing," I added, trying to get a little more bass in my voice.

Tony G was smoking and offered me a cigarette. I told him I didn't smoke and he said that was good. "A lot of people don't know it," he said, shaking my hand, "but cigarettes really aren't good for you."

We went outside and Jack pointed to a long black Chevrolet. It was fine and I felt pretty big-time climbing into the back. Henry sat next to me and Tony G climbed in last while Randy sat up front next to Jack.

"We don't combine record contracts with our club dates," Randy said as we pulled away from the curb.

"I don't blame you," Jack said. "We like to do everything with cash and a handshake so we don't do a lot of contracts."

"I can deal with cash," Randy said.

Cruising in the back of a Chevrolet through the streets of Harlem was what life was about in a very serious way. I had been down low but then I was back up and bounding with the hounds. All the way to the club I was thinking that these guys hadn't even heard us play our best. I figured we'd practice all day Saturday and be R-E-A-D-Y by Saturday night. I thought the first thing I was going to do with my part of the money was to buy myself a Chevrolet. I might even go for a Buick, I wasn't sure.

We pulled up to the corner of 128th and Lenox and Jack said we were at the club, but I didn't see any club.

"It's really high-class, but it's the kind of club you knock twice, tell them who sent you, and what the password is before they let you in," Jack said. "That's why I wanted you to see it before we came to an agreement. That okay with you? I think the boss is talking about some really good money."

"We can check it out," Henry said.

We walked into a door marked PARAMOUNT MOVING AND STORAGE. We went through the large office and into a much smaller office. There was a small desk and four chairs in the office and Jack took three of the chairs and put them against the wall.

"Why don't you boys sit down?" he said.

"Where's the club?" Randy asked.

"You'll see it soon enough," Jack said. "Maybe you can sing something for us while we wait for the boss."

"We don't sing," Randy said, looking around the office. "And we don't have all night to be fooling around here."

Tony G was thin and sort of pale. He actually looked a little as if he might be sick. He had a cough and I remembered what he had said about cigarettes. I thought he was reaching for a handkerchief when he dug into his pocket.

Wrong.

He touched the muzzle of a pistol against the bridge of Randy's nose. "Sit down and shut up," he said.

Randy's eyes got as big as saucers as he backed into the chair and sat down. Tony G pointed the gun toward me and Henry and we got into the other two chairs as fast as we could.

"We don't have any money," Henry said.

"I told you once to shut up." Tony G leaned toward us and spoke slowly. "I'm not going to tell you again."

My leg started shaking and my heart was jumping around in my chest. Randy was sniffing and I hoped he wouldn't start crying.

One hundred and twenty-eighth Street. My mind raced back to the night we had brought the truck back from New Jersey. I finally remembered where I had seen Jack. He was the one who gave Fats the money and told him to have Crab Cakes take the truck to the office.

Jack sat at the desk, took out a deck of cards, and started some game he was playing with himself. The man he called Tony G went out of the room.

"You think we can go home soon?" Henry asked.

Jack opened a desk drawer, pulled out another gun, and held it up so we could all see it. Then he looked me right in the eye and winked. "Ain't you glad I recognized you, sweetheart?"

What I really wanted to do, what I really, *really* wanted to do, was to pee. I remembered Mr. Mills and Tim Kelly saying how Dutch Schultz wouldn't mind killing me and

Henry. I figured he wouldn't know what to do with Randy except kill him just to keep things neat.

We sat there for about fifteen minutes more before the door opened again and Tony G came in, carrying a watermelon, followed by a short man wearing a hat. I recognized Dutch Schultz from his picture in the newspaper. Jack got up from the desk and swept the cards up. Tony G was coughing again as he pulled a chair up next to mine and put the watermelon on it.

"Here they are," Tony G said.

"They're musicians, just like the other one," Jack said.

Dutch Schultz looked over at us. "You know the sixth commandment?"

"Thou shalt not steal?" Henry asked.

"Tony, you got three bullets?"

"Yeah."

Schultz pointed toward the watermelon. The first time Tony shot the watermelon it bounced against the back of the chair and rolled onto the floor. That was when Henry started crying.

The second time he shot the watermelon it broke in two pieces. That was when Randy started to cry.

The third time he shot the biggest piece and sent it sliding along the floor. By then we were all crying.

"Tony, you got three more bullets?"

"Yeah."

That's when I started to pee. Not a lot. Just a little.

Tony G took a piece of paper out of the desk and made us write down our names and addresses.

"Now why don't you boys go on out of here and get what you owe me?" Schultz said.

Henry got up first and started walking stiff-legged toward the door. Then Randy got up and started easing out. I wanted to get up, too, but my legs didn't move.

"You ain't going?" Jack asked.

"Tony, you think he's telling us how tough he is?" Mr. Schultz asked.

I got up. I was crying a little and peeing a little. Just a little.

BAD NEWS AND DESPERATION BLUES AS I TAKE THE BUMPY ROAD TO A LIFE OF RECKLESS CRIME AND DEGRADATION.

My mama warned me about people like you."
Randy was still messed up when we reached
142nd Street. "Y'all look like you decent and
then I find out you ain't nothing but some bootleggers.
Now Dutch Schultz is going to kill me and I ain't even
done nothing."

"We didn't do anything, either," I said. "I told you
Crab Cakes took the truck. He's Fats's friend. Not ours."

"You and Henry were doing the bootlegging!" Randy
said. "You should have told me and I could have stayed
away from you."

"Man, I'll think of something," I said. "I'll get the
money up somehow."

"You better." Randy pointed a finger at me. "Or I'll
kill you myself."

I watched him go on down the street toward his house. There was no way I could blame him for being upset. When we were sitting in Dutch Schultz's office and watching that watermelon being shot I almost keeled over just from being that close to it.

The thing I was worried about was whether or not I should run out and find Fats and tell him what Dutch said. But I wasn't sure my legs were up to running anywhere.

When I got home, Mama was sitting in the kitchen and she asked me how we had done at the audition.

"Not too good," I said.

"Well, that just could be the Lord's way of sending you a message," she said.

"Yes, ma'am."

"Because your uncle Cephus called this morning to officially offer you the chance of working for him," Mama said. "He said you — Boy, did you wet your pants?"

"A kid sprayed me with a hose," I said.

"Yeah, okay." Mama was looking sideways, meaning she didn't believe me. "Anyway, he said you have to make up your mind if you want a real opportunity and a true career."

"Yes, ma'am."

"So what should I tell him?" she asked.

"That I'm working on making up my mind," I said. "I was thinking about going to college, too."

That's not what Mama wanted to hear, but it would have to do until I thought of something else.

Matt was sitting up in bed trying to look intelligent and stinking up the room with his pipe.

"You have to put that thing out," I said. "It's bothering my allergy."

"I don't think you really have an allergy," he said. "I think it's all in your head."

I put my robe on quickly and then pulled my pants down. What a mess.

"Say, Matt." I stretched across my bed. "What would you do if you owed a big-time gangster a lot of money? Do you think he would take it a few dollars at a time?"

"If you owed money to the mob you'd have to pay interest on it," Matt said. "You'd probably end up paying four or five times what you owed at the start."

"How about just going to the police?"

"Rat him out to the cops?" Matt put the pipe down and turned onto one elbow. "If it was someone like Bumpy Johnson, who's probably the biggest black mobster in the city next to Caspar Holstein, then he would really be mad. He'd probably shoot you, cut your body up, throw you in the river, then fish you out so he could do it all over again. The worse thing in the world to do is to rat out a gangster because they have guys who will come after you. Anyway, what do you care? You don't owe anybody any money, do you?"

"No, but a friend of mine does."

"Who?"

"You don't know him," I said. "Guy plays piano over at the Lafayette Theater."

"Fats? Big Fats with the roll-y eyes?"

"Yeah."

"He owes everybody money," Matt said. "I heard he owes Bumpy Johnson a few hundred. Bumpy don't care because he likes the way Fats plays."

I remembered that Dutch Schultz hadn't said anything about shooting Fats. Maybe he liked the way he played, too. Meanwhile, I got another good idea. I'd borrow some money from Bumpy Johnson to pay off Dutch Schultz and then pay off Bumpy a little bit at a time if he liked the way I played, too, which I figured he probably would once he heard me. Bumpy walked on the shady side of the street. He also owned a pest extermination business, and hired all the drunks and down-and-outers who needed a few dollars. They said he was mean, but I never heard about him killing anybody. I was going to ask Matt where Bumpy Johnson lived, but I didn't want him all up in my business. I just had to figure a way to talk to Bumpy as soon as possible.

Got my hair cut Saturday. Ralph's Barbershop on Lenox Avenue was crowded when I got there and Little Pete, the

Cuban guy who took numbers and kept the place clean, was having an argument with OK Taylor about whether a chicken only laid white eggs or sometimes it could lay white eggs and sometimes brown eggs.

"One hen can't lay two different-color eggs," Pete was saying.

"You talking about Cuban hens," OK said. He was already standing in the doorway ready to get the last word in. "An American hen is twice as smart as a Cuban hen and can lay any color egg it wants to lay. Now deal with that!"

He closed the door so he didn't hear the other guys in the barbershop agree that he didn't know what he was talking about.

"Where he get a name like OK, anyway?" A brown-skinned man was getting a shave.

"His mama had so many kids she ran out of names," Ray said. "When he come along they just called him the Other Kid. Then they shortened that to OK."

That was pretty funny and everybody laughed. There were some more jokes passed around and everybody was joining in. Then I asked, in a casual kind of way, if anybody knew where Bumpy Johnson lived. Ralph stopped cutting hair and gave me a look.

"Boy, you don't want to know where Bumpy lives," he said. "You don't want to know a thing about Bumpy that you don't have to know."

I didn't say anything more about Bumpy Johnson and nobody said anything more to me.

I really wasn't sure how much Dutch Schultz wanted to shoot me. But I was very sure that I did not want to be shot so I knew I needed to come up with at least part of the money he said I owed him. I figured I could get Fats to come up with part of the money. Matt had said that Fats owed everybody money and nobody seemed to be in a hurry to shoot him. But he had a good job at the Lafayette and he also made records once in a while so maybe they thought he would be able to pay them off after a while. What I really needed was a better-paying job.

"How hard is it to write a whole book?" I asked Langston Hughes when he came to the office.

"Langston, don't even bother answering him," Miss Fauset said. "I don't think Mark could write a whole grocery list."

Langston smiled his little crooked smile and went on with his business with Miss Fauset, but when he finished he came back over to where I was putting our new advertising rates for colleges in envelopes.

"Writing a book isn't all that hard," Langston said. "If you plan it out you can do it. The hard thing is to get someone to publish it."

"You make a lot of money from a book?"

"I never saw a rich Negro writer," Langston said. "Maybe you can pay your rent once in a while, but that's about it. One time I figured out I could make more money shining shoes than polishing up my poetry. I just don't like working outdoors."

"You think I could learn to write poetry?"

"Sure. I used to copy other people's poems and rewrite them," Langston said. "That gave me a feel for what it was like."

"How do you know what to write about?" I asked.

"Most of the time I'll write about whatever interests me at the moment. I'll be going to that rent party I told you about, maybe I'll write about that. You still want to come?"

He fished out a square of colored paper with the address on it. Under the address it read GET-IN FEE, 25¢.

"I'll be there," I said.

Langston was a nice guy and I thought about what he said. Writing was something I could do in my spare time when I wasn't playing. The way I figured, I was learning enough stuff working at *The Crisis* that I could keep myself busy if I put my mind to it and if Dutch Schultz didn't do anything drastic. I remembered seeing one of Langston's poems in the magazine and I looked it up. Miss Fauset asked me what I was doing and I told her I was going to copy down Langston's poem and rewrite it so I could learn poetry. She got that little twitch in the corner of her mouth the way she does sometimes when she doesn't believe me.

Langston's poem was called "The Negro Looks at Rivers." I wrote the whole thing down, then I rewrote it as Langston said. I liked what I wrote and decided to show it to Miss Fauset.

— The Negro Looks at Livers —

I've known livers
I've known livers as old as the world and filled
With human blood
My soul is as old as my liver

I've known fat men who could make their livers quiver
I've known skinny men with nothing but a sliver of a liver
I know a German who eats onions with his liver
I saw a man drowning his liver in the river

I've known livers
Squishy, bloody livers
My soul is as old as my liver

Miss Fauset made a face as if reading the poem hurt her. She didn't need to do that. Anyway, I agreed with Langston that writing poems is probably not a way to make a lot of money. Not in a hurry, anyway.

I told Matt that I was going to meet Henry and Randy to practice hymns to try out for Sunday services.

"Don't tell Mama," I told him.

So when she asked me where I was going with a clean shirt on after seven o'clock and I told her I was thinking about dropping off at the Thursday night prayer meeting I knew Mr. Mouth Almighty Matt would be ready.

"I think he's going to be practicing sax with his friends so they can play in church," he said, a stupid grin on his stupid face.

"Well, at least he's thinking about the Lord," Mama said, smiling.

Which was why I loved Mama!

I called Randy and Henry and asked them if they wanted to go to the rent party and they both said no. Henry said he had to do something with his mother but Randy went on about how he was thinking maybe I was just a hoodlum or something.

"They will probably be shooting and cutting people just to pass the time of day!" he said.

I was a little jumpy about going out into the street at night, but I was just as worried about staying home. At least if I went to the party I could take my mind off of Dutch Schultz and the watermelons for a little while.

I got to the rent party, which was held at 39 West 132nd Street. It was a brownstone and there was a note pointing to one bell that read PARTY. Also, there was a regular printed sign that said NO LOUD TALKING, NO SITTING ON THE STOOP, NO LOUD MUSIC, AND NO ACTING COLORED.

I paid the quarter at the door to get in. Most of the people at the party were black but Mr. Van Vechten, the man I had seen at the party at Mr. Knopf's house, was also there. There was also a white woman sitting with a black man on one of the couches.

The first time I heard about rent parties it was Mr. Mills passing out pieces of paper with his address on it. I asked him what a rent party was.

"Every month there's a race between the first of the month and payday and the winner gets to deal with the sidewalk. When payday comes first and you can pay your rent, then everything is sweet and neat and you can come out of your house and laugh at the sidewalk or even spit on it if you have a mind. But if the first of the month comes around and you ain't got the rent money and the sidewalk is looking at you and grinning, then you got to get yourself a rent party going.

"You charge a quarter at the door, then you charge for the food — maybe some ribs and a pot of greens or some hopping john, then you charge for the drinks. Now if you can make yourself a whole bathtub full of some gin that don't make you go blind or some rye that don't burn your throat out, you can make enough money to pay your rent.

Naturally you got to have some entertainment so the folks will dance and need to eat something and sweat enough so they need to drink something, too. When a rent party gets right, I mean really gets right, it's like testifying to the Lord! Only this time it's the landlord."

The party was already going and the room was too crowded to see who all was there, but soon as I heard the piano I knew who was playing. It was Fats. I really wanted to see him to tell him what had happened with Dutch Schultz. There was also a trumpet player, a skinny guy on sax, and a strange-looking banjo player who kept blinking in time with the music. I liked that.

The music was loud and good, and everybody who had more than one leg was on the floor dancing. There was all kinds of loud talking, loud music, and loud-acting Colored. People were bumping into each other but nobody seemed to mind. A table against the wall was set up like a bar and a short wide man with all gold front teeth was selling drinks.

I knew that selling liquor had been illegal since 1918 but there was so much whiskey going around the room that I wondered if I was the only one who knew it.

Mr. Van Vechten tried dancing with one of the girls and people laughed at him, but he didn't mind and they didn't seem to mind so I asked a girl to dance with me.

She asked me how old I was and I told her I was nineteen and she said she was, too, but I thought she was younger.

We did the Lindy Hop and then a slow dance and Louise, which was her name, said she was hungry and that we should buy something to eat.

I had brought three dollars with me and the plates of food — collard greens, a black-eyed-beans-and-rice dish called hopping john, fried chicken, and biscuits — only cost fifty cents each so that was all right. It was some kind of good, too.

The music might have been the best I had ever heard. Fats was wailing and Mr. Van Vechten asked him to hold still for a minute while he took his picture. People were getting out of the way of the camera, and Fats started playing the piano and singing about folks ducking and hiding and I loved that. Langston showed up and I went up and said hello to him.

"This is what gives Harlem its pulse," Langston said. "Fast music, fast dancing, and living fast enough to stay ahead of the blues and the landlord."

"This is real life, the way it's supposed to be," I said.

"You think this is real life?" Langston looked at me from the side of his eyes.

"Yeah," I said. "This is just the way I would like to spend every night."

Langston looked away and I looked to see what he was watching, but his eyes had just sort of glazed over. Then he turned back to me and smiled. "This is a kind of real," he said. "A hot slice of life that's very attractive. It's so sassy, and the rhythm of it is so familiar you think it's the only way to live. But there are other faces and other places you can call real."

"This one is good enough for me," I said.

He laughed and hit my elbow with his hand before sliding through the crowd toward the other side of the room. I liked Langston. A lot.

Fats Waller danced with the white girl, and the black man she was with got mad. When the dance was over, Fats started making up a song about her and that made her man even madder, especially when everyone started laughing at him. Then Fats made up a song about the man. He called it "Eat Some Sherbert, Herbert, and Stay Cool."

When Fats took a break I sat down next to him and told him about meeting Dutch Schultz and the watermelons getting shot.

"Don't you hate it when people get that serious about their little lives?" Fats asked. "Why can't they just enjoy themselves?"

"I do, but I don't want to get shot because I'm not a watermelon," I said. "Watermelons don't mind getting shot."

"You got something there," Fats said. "I never heard

about a watermelon worrying about being shot or anything else. I'll go over and see him the first thing in the
morning."

Fats was smiling and patting my hand but I knew that
he was not going to go over and see Dutch in the morning.
What he was going to do was play his music and have a
good time and hope nothing caught up to him.

"How you know him?" Louise asked me.

"We hang out together sometimes," I said, which was
not exactly a to-a-tee lie.

Fats Waller was playing the kind of music I wanted to
play, full of fun and rhythm. I didn't drink but everyone
else was drinking and dancing and having a good time. I
hadn't been sure that I wanted to come to the party, but by
the time it was winding down, I knew what I wanted to do
with the rest of my life: play hot music at jazz clubs and
rent parties. I had tried writing a poem and Miss Fauset
didn't think too much of it, but even if she had, it had not
been that exciting, not as exciting as playing my saxophone,
or even as exciting as eating fried chicken and collard greens
and not nearly as exciting as dancing with Louise.

Louise gave me her address and told me she would sure
like to see me again and then she kissed me right in the
middle of the floor. The lights had been turned down so
not too many people saw us but by that time I didn't even

care. Louise had a job in a button factory down on 32nd Street and had to get home early.

"And I live with my mother, and you know what that means," she said. "You got your own place?"

"I'm looking for an apartment now," I said.

When Louise left, the party was definitely slowing down and they were bringing the coats out of the bedroom. That's when Fats called me over and introduced me to Bumpy Johnson.

Bumpy was short and mean-looking. He was real dark and talked like one of those fast-talking Negroes from South Carolina that Daddy called "Geechies."

"Fats said you need some money." He looked at me as if he was mad about something.

"Yes, I do," I said.

"Be on the 125th Street pier tomorrow night at eight," he said. "I got a delivery coming in. Don't be late."

He turned and walked away before I could answer. There was a bump on the back of his head but I didn't run behind him and say anything to him about it or anything else, either. Fats was putting on his coat. There were two women with him, one on each arm. I was scared of Dutch Schultz. I was scared of Jack, Dutch's man. I was scared of Tony G. And now I was scared of Bumpy Johnson. All that scared was on the left side of my brain. The rent party, swinging and singing and dancing with Louise, was on the right side of my brain, and everything in the middle was just jelly on the griddle.

When I got home I opened the door as quietly as I could. I saw the apartment was dark and slipped out of my shoes and moved along close to the wall so the floorboards would not creak. Everything was fine until I got into my room. Who was sleeping on my bed? Right! Mama! If I woke her up I was going to have to explain where I had been, who I was with, and why I was coming home so late.

I settled on the couch and figured out how many ways I could get myself in trouble without even trying. I said a prayer and told God that if He got me out of this one I would keep myself straight.

"This time I really mean it, too." I prayed.

I knew Mama was going to ask me a hundred questions about where I had been and what I had been doing and before I was halfway through explaining how I used to work for Dutch Schultz and was now working for Bumpy Johnson she would be telling Jesus how she was ready to go on up to heaven because she couldn't do anything more with me down here on Earth. I felt sorry for Mama having to worry and everything, but I needed to let Jesus know I wasn't exactly ready to go to heaven anytime soon.

THE SAD DAY WHEN I EMBARK ON A LIFE OF CRIME, AM FORCED TO ADMIT IT, BUT THEREBY BECOME A BIG HIT WITH THE SASSIEST LADY THIS SIDE OF SWEET PARADISE.

As I walked past the milk-processing plant on 125th Street I slowed down to watch the bottles on the conveyor belt fill with the white liquid. The bottles were all the same, all waiting to go out into the world and into the homes of honest and good people. I was on my way to meet Bumpy Johnson and sink into the underworld.

"Why I got to come with you?" Henry said. "You already got me into trouble one time. Now what's going to happen? Dutch Schultz is going to shoot me and Bumpy Johnson is going to shoot me."

"We're going to straight up work for Bumpy and then we'll get paid and take the money over to Dutch Schultz as a down payment," I said. "Don't worry, I got it all figured out."

"Yeah, that watermelon had it all figured out, too," Henry said. "Look, Fats is your friend. He's not my friend."

"You want to leave?" I asked. "Then go on and leave. But since you are my ace I'm going to try to save you from Dutch Schultz even if I have to risk my own life to do it."

Henry sucked his teeth, rolled his eyes at me, then did a sharp turn, and started walking east. My heart sank a little but I knew I had to get some money from somewhere so I took a deep breath and headed again for the pier. When Henry caught up with me I didn't say anything, but I was glad to see his butt.

"This your boy?" Bumpy asked, nodding his head toward Henry.

"Yeah."

Bumpy grunted and told us to follow him. We went over and sat on the edge of the wooden pier. There were some old guys crabbing off the side, and one was pulling his trap up. The trap was square with fish bait tied to the bottom. When it was pulled up, the sides trapped any crabs inside. There were no crabs in the trap when the man pulled it up, so he tossed it back into the Hudson.

"Here comes the boat," Bumpy said.

I looked out and saw a small fishing boat moving slowly toward the pier.

"Do what the old man tells you," Bumpy was growling now.

I didn't know who the old man was and Bumpy didn't give me a chance to answer. He walked toward the street and got into a low-slung car. I could feel my heart racing.

The man crabbing turned toward where Henry and me were standing and beckoned us over.

We got to him just as the boat pulled along the pier. Two dark figures on the boat started hauling out wooden crates and handing them up to the old man who had climbed down the side of the pier onto a kind of ledge. He grabbed the crates and handed them up to me. I didn't know what to do, so I took them and started piling them on the pier.

When the truck pulled up, lights out and motor purring smooth as a pussycat, it all looked good. Henry and me loaded the truck, putting the last two crates in the cab. The driver, who had a West Indian accent and was a minute-to-midnight black told us to get in front.

The old man who had been crabbing was standing outside the truck. He put his hand to his head in a kind of salute and we were on our way across town. For a moment I feel relieved to be away from the pier. For a moment. We had barely crossed Old Broadway when we heard the sirens.

The driver never slowed down, he just pulled in behind one of the police cars and we headed uptown. All I could think of was the 135th Street Precinct but we went past 135th and even farther. When the truck stopped, a cop stuck his head in the back of the truck and told us to get out. A light summer rain had started, and we walked through it as we were herded into 232 West 147th Street.

I couldn't think as I walked up the stairs. Not one single thought came into my mind except I was in big trouble. What I figured was that we were being taken to Dutch's house and we were going to get killed at least twice apiece. My mind was telling my legs to run but my legs weren't listening, just going slowly up the stairs.

The first policeman, a heavyset red-faced guy with a potbelly, banged on a door. The peephole opened, and then the door. A short, Colored man who looked as if he was wearing makeup opened the door and looked us over. Then he stepped aside and the police pushed me, Henry, and the driver inside.

The apartment smelled of incense and liniment and I thought I was going to get sick.

"Queenie, look what we found coming from the river," one of the policemen said.

I looked up and saw a tall woman, the exact color of a Brazil nut, standing in the doorway of her parlor. She was wearing a bright, silky-type skirt and a blouse with sleeves you could see through. She also wore big silver earrings and a gold comb on one side of her head.

"Aren't you boys up past your bedtime?" Queenie asked in a voice that was just a little deeper than mine.

"Don't be snooty," a short, dark-haired policeman said. "We could arrest you all."

"No, you can't, darling," Queenie said. "We all have too much at stake to be foolish. Now don't we? Is anybody hungry?"

The next thing I knew the woman they were calling Queenie had called in another woman, fat and pleasant-looking, who smiled at everybody and served sandwiches and iced tea. After all of us had eaten, Queenie gave out envelopes to the policemen and they left. Bumpy was sitting in the corner, scowling.

"Don't look so big-eyed, it's how business is done in New York." Queenie reached over and ran her fingers under my chin. "Bumpy, are these boys supposed to be employees or did you mean to adopt them?"

"They did a job for the Dutchman," Bumpy said. "That was the load that disappeared."

"You know about that?" Henry asked.

"He hires amateurs, that's why he gets burned," Queenie said. "How's your math? Can you multiply three hundred sixty-seven times twenty-four for me right quick?"

"What were those numbers?" I asked, fishing around my pockets looking for a pencil.

"You just failed the test," Queenie said. "You could

never run numbers for me if you can't even remember two at a time. What did Dutch say to you when his liquor disappeared?"

"He shot a watermelon," Henry said.

"Oh, that's a threat." Queenie waved a long finger in front of her face. "Queenie doesn't like threats. He should have just gone on and shot you. Don't you think so?"

"No, ma'am."

"I would have shot you," Queenie said. "You probably won't be able to get the money up, so there's no reason to threaten you, isn't that right?"

"They were working with that piano player, Fats," Bumpy said. "I think he didn't want to shoot him."

"Oh, people are just so *particular* these days," Queenie said.

"You wouldn't want to loan us the money and let us pay you back, would you?" Henry asked.

Queenie turned and looked at me dead in the eye. "Honey, there ain't enough to you to make a good sandwich and you're trying to make a business deal with Queenie?"

"We just thought it might be a good idea," I said. "That way maybe Dutch won't shoot us."

"I don't know why he didn't shoot you the first time," Queenie said. "Giving people breaks when they mess with your money is not good business. Any fool knows that. But, you know, maybe I *will* lend you the money. There could be something in it for me if people knew that I gave you two sardines a break."

"Nah, they ain't nothing but some trouble," Bumpy said. "They're young and stupid. Probably get themselves killed before you get your money back."

"We'll try not to get killed," I heard Henry saying.

"Bumpy, if we get Dutch's money back, then who does the liquor belong to?" Queenie was wearing long dangly earrings and put the tip of her fingernail through one of them as she spoke. "And if the liquor belongs to us, I think I can find a good use for it."

"They ain't nothing but a jinx, Queenie," Bumpy said. "They've lost Dutch's stash and now they got picked up by the police."

"Or, we can put out a rumor that they stole Dutch's liquor and sold it to us," Queenie said. "Then he'd have to shoot them and we could call Mayor Hylan and give him all the details. Dutch will have to get out of Harlem and set up shop someplace else. Then we'd have the numbers all to ourselves. All we have to do is to make sure that the police find their bodies."

"If he does shoot them he'll probably toss them in the river." This from the fat woman who had served the sandwiches. "He doesn't have any imagination."

"Do both of you float?" Queenie asked.

Henry started crying again. I was determined not to cry and tried to clear my throat to say something, but nothing came out.

"Why don't you boys go on home, now," Queenie said. "Bumpy and I will think it over. And do keep your mouths shut."

Bumpy put some bills in my pocket and some in Henry's and walked us to the door.

"How we going to know what's going to happen?" Henry asked.

"If somebody shoots you, you'll be able to figure it all out by who's doing the shooting," was Bumpy's answer.

By the time we got downstairs and onto the street Henry was crying again. He was the cryingest guitar player I had ever met and I told him so.

"I'm not used to being scared all the time, man," he said.

"Look at it this way, Henry." I put my arm around him. "Things could be worse."

"How?"

That was a good question and I told him I would think on it.

"You think we're going to be okay?" he asked.

"No."

It was past eleven when I left Henry. I knew Mama was going to be up and ready. I wasn't even worried. There was nothing she could do to me that a half dozen other people weren't ready to do worse. I got home and opened the door, and Mama was at the kitchen table talking to some woman. She looked a little familiar.

"It's nice of you to drop by," Mama said. "Why don't you say hello to your cousin, Mrs. McKinney?"

"How do you do, ma'am?" I remembered her visiting about two years before. She had brought her little girl along.

"She was waiting for you because I had told her how much you had grown," Mama said, her voice getting harder. "I didn't tell her how disrespectful you had become since you started smelling your own pee. Just walking in any-time you feel like it."

"Oh, Ginny, boys love to have fun." This from Mrs. McKinney.

"Your cousin's very respectful daughter is in the living room," Mama said. "She was just out in Hollywood, California, and was in a movie. That's what she's been doing with her time. Why don't you go and speak to her before you leave. Or did you plan to spend the night?"

"I'm spending the night, Mama," I answered.

I went into the living room and found Mrs. McKinney's daughter reading *House & Garden*. She looked up at me and my heart stopped dead in my chest. She had grown in all the right places and was a class-A knockout.

"Hi!" Me.

"I heard your mother giving it to you," she said. "Don't worry, I get it all the time!"

"You've grown up. . . ."

"Nina Mae."

"You've grown up, Nina Mae," I managed.

"Your mother said you play saxophone." Nina's eyes were dark and wide and I could feel myself falling in. "Were you playing tonight?"

"Yeah, at Small's," I said. I don't know where that came from.

"You look really tired."

"Well, I have a few problems," I said. I sat next to her on the couch. Suddenly, I felt as if I were a hundred years old. "I owe a guy some money," I said. "His name is Dutch Schultz and —"

"The gangster?" Her eyes got wider and she leaned toward me.

"And I tried to get some of the money tonight by working with another bootlegger, but we got picked up by the cops."

"That's so exciting!"

"It's not that exciting when Dutch Schultz's arm man shoots a watermelon right next to me and my guys and says he has three more bullets for us."

"That is so front-page I could die!" Nina Mae said, her big beautiful eyes getting bigger and more beautiful.

"Don't tell anybody!" I said. "I don't want to get you involved."

"Cross my heart," she promised, taking my hand in hers and crossing her heart with my fingertips.

"Nina Mae, I'm ready to go," her mother called.

"Your mother has our number," Nina Mae whispered. "Get it and call me. You are so front-page!"

She kissed me on the cheek, jumped up, and started for the door. She stopped, turned in the doorway, and gave me a smile that burst in my head like a dozen Roman candles shooting off all at once.

I knew I would be in love with her forever if I wasn't dead first. Lying in the darkness I put my arms around my pillow. Nina Mae was right, life could be interesting when you were front-page material.

■ ■ ■ ■ ■ ■ ■ ■ ■ ■ ■ ■ ■ ■ ■ ■ ■ ■ ■ ■

I ASK THE GOOD LORD TO SAVE ME FROM A LIFE OF CRIME AND I AM SAVED! AND SAVED AGAIN! AND AGAIN! WOE IS ME.

■ ■ ■ ■ ■ ■ ■ ■ ■ ■ ■ ■ ■ ■ ■ ■ ■ ■ ■

Nina Mae had been impressed by my life jigging in the underworld, but I was getting tired of it. I was scared to walk down the street. I was scared every time I saw a policeman. Scared of white guys because they might be part of Dutch Schultz's mob ready to take me to him or even shoot me, and now I was scared of black guys who might be in Queenie's gang.

Friday night came and I didn't even want to go out but I didn't have a choice, our apartment felt like an oven. I went downstairs about midnight and the stoop was full of people trying to escape the heat. A couple of people had brought milk crates out and sat on them as they fanned themselves. Above us there were people sleeping on the fire escapes. Old Man Mills had brought out a tub filled with ice and was wrapping pieces of it in his handkerchief and putting it on the back of his neck.

"That help much?" Jimmy Key asked.

"Yeah, it helps a lot," Old Man Mills said. "It's like when you baking a chicken and baste it in its own juices just before it's done. You notice when you do that how pleased that chicken looks?"

It was just as hot on the stoop as it was in my room but every once in a while the air did move a little and make you think there was going to be a breeze. The breeze never did come and one by one we all went upstairs. I vowed to myself right then and there that as soon as I got rich I was going to buy a fan for every room in my house.

Saturday morning I met Henry in Mount Morris Park.

"This fast life is too much for me," I said. "What I need is some peace and quiet."

"We'll be going back to school in a week or so," Henry answered. "I never thought I'd look forward to school, but I do."

"I have decided that I'm going to be a New Negro after all," I said. "Maybe write some poems and play symphonies. You know what I mean?"

"Symphonies? You can't get away from hot music when it's in your blood like it's in ours," Henry said. "If we tried to play some kind of symphony it would probably come out swinging. All we need to do is get ourselves out of this mess and get back to being us again."

I gave Henry a look because I didn't know he was that wise. What he said made a lot of sense. If we could just squeeze our way out of the clutches of Dutch Schultz we would be back on top and in the groove.

"You have any ideas?" I asked.

"No, but my grandmother said if things get really rough out in the world you should pray," Henry said. "That's what I did. I got down on my knees and asked God not to let Dutch Schultz shoot me. I think you ought to do the same thing."

"How about Bumpy Johnson and Queenie?" I asked.

"You think they're serious?" Henry nudged me and nodded toward two fine-looking girls walking arm in arm through the park.

"Bumpy had a pistol in his pocket," I said. "I saw the handle sticking out. Is that serious enough for you?"

"Okay, so tonight before I go to bed I'll pray that he don't get me, either," Henry said. "You know, Mark, at the beginning of summer I was getting really tired of being a teenager, having my parents telling me what to do. I wanted some being on my own. Now I'm not so sure."

We watched a few kids playing in the park and then walked over to La Marketa on Park Avenue and looked around there. Henry was quiet and I knew he was thinking. I was, too. When it got near eleven he said he had to head uptown and he left and I drifted back across 125th Street.

I was walking slow and easy but my head was doing double duty in the thinking department about some of the things I had learned.

Miss Fauset was always talking about the New Negro, but I was seeing that there were a whole lot of different kinds of people in the world. The thing was they were all so different. There were people like Miss Fauset and Dr. DuBois and Miss Newsome, dealing with the magazine and stories and poems; then there were people like Dutch and Bumpy and Queenie, who were doing a whole different kind of thing and liking what they were doing. Then there were my parents and Old Man Mills who were just pushing from day to day and hoping for a better life down the line. And there was Fats, having a good old time every day and not minding what kind of trouble he got into, and Langston Hughes, who probably never got into trouble and was having a good time writing his poems. With so many kinds of people around I didn't know how anyone could make a decision as to which one they wanted to be. The thing was, there might even be people somewhere living in a way that I would like even better, and I just hadn't met them yet.

When I got home, Lavinia was over. She and Matt were in the living room acting stupid and he was playing what he was calling "ragtime" but it sounded more like "raggedy time" to me. I couldn't see how a black man could be born without any rhythm at all, but that was Matt for you.

I went to bed and lay down in the dark, shut my eyes, and said a prayer. I asked God to get me out of trouble with anybody I was in trouble with and I didn't mention anybody by name because I figured He knew who was after me, but I did say I needed saving three times. When I finished my prayer I felt good. I also knew that since Henry had made the same prayer it wouldn't be a big deal for God to double up the protection.

"Mark! You in here?" Mama jerked on the overhead light just as I was dozing off.

"What's wrong?" I asked.

"I don't know!" she answered. "But a boy just delivered a telegram for you."

"You sure that's not for me?" Matt was standing in the doorway. "The school was supposed to notify me if I got a scholarship."

Mama was tearing open the telegram, and Matt was trying to read it over her shoulder.

"'I have paid Dutch Schultz for you/ stop. Now you owe me the money/ stop. You will pay it or/ stop. Madame Stephanie St. Clair.'"

"Who is Stephanie St. Clair?" Matt asked.

"What money are they talking about?" Mama's voice was getting higher and higher. "And what you know about some Dutch Schultz?"

I knew Madame Stephanie St. Claire must have been

Queenie and that God was moving in mysterious ways to get me out of trouble. I didn't want to complicate things for Him so I did some fast thinking.

"I owed Mr. Dutch — Mr. Schultz some money and I asked Miss St. Claire to lend it to me and —"

"Dutch Schultz who you read about in the papers?" Mama asked.

"Sort of . . . yeah."

"Sort of? *Sort of?*" Her voice was getting higher and higher. "Mark, what are you doing owing money to some criminal you read about in the newspapers!"

"I was throwing rocks in the park and one of them broke his car window," I said. I don't even know where that came from. I just felt my lips moving and that's what came out.

Mama was crying and asking the Lord to help her in her hour of need and saying how she was a churchgoing woman and did not deserve what was going on. Then she asked me how much money I owed Mr. Schultz and I told her $22. I didn't like to lie to Mama but I was on a roll and they were just coming.

"I will go to your uncle Cephus to see if he will lend me the money," she said. "But Mark, let me tell you this. You have found my one good nerve and you are working it down to a twitch! Do you hear me, boy? A twitch!"

"Yes, ma'am."

Mama was shaking her head and calling out to the Lord as she left the room. I hoped she wasn't mucking up my prayers.

Mama woke me up first thing Sunday morning and told me to take a bath. "You are going to church with me," she said. "I have been so worried about sending Matt to college I've been neglecting your upbringing. That's going to stop. Get yourself ready for some direct communicating with the Lord!"

I knew that was a sign. I had asked the Lord to get me out of trouble and He had. Now Mama was taking me to church, and I knew when I got there I would thank the Lord and we would be square. I figured He knew that Queenie would not hurt me and I would figure a way to pay her off. In fact, maybe He even had a way for me to get the money without having to work too hard.

They turned on the fans at Abyssinian Baptist Church long before the people arrived for Sunday morning services so that by the time we got there it was pretty cool inside. I was as clean as a new nickel, and Mama had made me wear Matt's suit. Matt said he would be along later but I knew he wouldn't because Lavinia was Catholic and he would probably be running down to St. Joseph's on 125th Street. So it was just me, Mama, and Daddy. She got him, too, even though he said his foot wouldn't fit into his good shoes. He came in his old shoes, limping a little and saying the Lord delivered the Children of Israel *from* pain, not *into* pain.

If the Lord was going to hang out somewhere in Harlem it would have to be at the Abyssinian Baptist. From the outside it looked great, almost like the old cathedrals you saw in magazines. Inside it was even better with the stained-glass windows and the pews lined up just right and that big organ up front. But what made it really special were the ladies in their Sunday hats. There were small hats that some of the younger women and girls wore but the best ones were the older women who wore the big hats. Some of them had flowers and most of them had lace and feathers. One big lady had a hat that was high on one side and came down nearly to her shoulder on the other. Those ladies were making a joyful noise unto the Lord when they sang but they were looking good, too.

Reverend Powell usually had some part of the service where you were supposed to thank God for all of your blessings so I waited for that to come so I could tell Him I was grateful. The Abyssinian choir was the best la-de-da choir in Harlem and they sang two good songs and then we all sang a song. Sister Ellis gave a short report and then Reverend Powell asked her to read from John 2, where Christ started doing his miracles.

Reverend Powell was just getting warmed up when the

dog started barking. People started turning their heads and looking around and a couple of the deacons got up and headed down the aisle.

"Mister, you can't bring a dog in here!" It was Deacon Little. "Don't you know this is a church?"

"I'm just looking for Mark Purvis," was the answer, with the "Mark Purvis" as loud as it could come out of his mouth.

"You have to wait until the services are over and you have to wait outside!" another man said.

I turned and saw Crab Cakes pulling on his dog's leash. The bigheaded bulldog was growling at one of the deacons.

"Mark, tell me he is not looking for you." Mama sounded a little like she was going to cry. "Please tell me that."

"What you want?" I called to Crab Cakes.

"I got your whiskey outside," he called back across a row of sisters who looked like they were all going to pass out at the same time. "The whole truckload."

Two nurses were fanning Mama when me and Daddy and Crab Cakes went outside. People I didn't even know were shaking their heads and making clucking noises and I heard Reverend Powell saying how they would pray for our Negro youth.

"Where have you been, man?" I asked outside.

"I went to Baltimore to get Abby," Crab Cakes said. "Me and Abby been together all our lives. I told you I couldn't stand being away from him and he can't stand being away from me."

Abby looked at me and gave out a low growl that must have meant something like "What you got to say about it?" I didn't have nothing to say but then it came to me that what had happened was that the Lord had saved me from Queenie and Bumpy by bringing back the whiskey. The Lord knew what He was doing.

"Okay, now this is what you got to do," I said to Crab Cakes. "Take this over to Queenie's house and tell her —"

"I been over there," Crab Cakes said. "I took it up to Dutch Schultz's place and he said he sold it to Queenie. Then I took it over to Queenie's house and she said she paid for it but it's getting too hot for her so it belongs to you now. But Dutch, he wants his truck back and he said I better get it back to him quick. So I brought the whiskey over to you and we can unload it right here so I can get the truck back."

"You can't unload a truckload of whiskey in front of Abyssinian Baptist Church!" Deacon Little had come outside to see what was going on and had been listening to the whole thing.

"Everybody calm down," Daddy said. "I know where we can take it. Get into the truck."

Daddy, Crab Cakes, and Abby got into the cab of the truck and I had to sit in the back. I didn't know where we were going but I was beginning to suspect that the Lord hadn't got everything just right. Yet.

We pulled up in front of the Cotton Club, and Daddy rang the bell. Petey Jones answered the bell, and Daddy told him that we needed to store some whiskey in the club for a few days.

"I don't know," Petey said.

"Petey, the club is closed down so nobody is going to know and there's three dollars in it for you," Daddy said.

The three dollars did it for Petey and that's how me and Daddy and Crab Cakes got to unloading the truck of bootleg whiskey into the Cotton Club. When we finished, Crab Cakes and Abby took off for Dutch's place with the truck.

"Now what is all this about?" Daddy asked.

I told him the whole story and he just groaned and groaned the whole way through it.

"I'll start asking around tomorrow to see where we can sell this whiskey," Daddy said. "Mark, you are a young black man. Sometimes, living here in Harlem, we walk on the sunny side of the street and sometimes we walk on the shady side. I know that because I've been black a whole lot longer than you. Anything you've seen — I've lived. But I also know that you got to be careful on both sides of the street. I've spent my whole life stepping lightly, praying nightly, and knowing when to cut bait and run. It's time for you to cut bait and get to footing!"

"Yes, sir, but I owe this money to Queenie . . ."

"Boy, I will start asking around tomorrow to see where we can sell this whiskey," Daddy said. "In the meantime, please don't say nothing to your mama that's going to give her a heart attack. Please don't do that."

"Yes, sir."

When I got home, Mama took one look at me and started crying. Every time Daddy looked at me he hung his head and shook it like he was mourning. I stayed in my room all afternoon and kept quiet. But in my heart I was feeling good. When Daddy found somebody to sell the bootleg whiskey to I could pay off Queenie and then I wouldn't owe anybody anything.

I also made a decision not to get myself involved any more with hoodlums and gangsters and stick to playing in clubs and for rent parties. Life was not going to be easy for the New Negro saxophone player, but I knew I would give it my best. I was even thinking of how I was going to call Louise and Nina Mae and tell them the whole story, although I knew Nina Mae would probably appreciate it more.

I felt so good going to work Monday that even Miss Fauset noticed it. But then she got into how different people were either doing good things for black people or bad things.

"Paul Robeson is going to play *The Emperor Jones* on the London stage while some fool named Johnny Hudgins is going to appear in blackface on Broadway," she said. "Now who do you think is going to do more for the Negro race?"

I got that one right.

When I got home, Daddy said that he might be able to sell the whiskey to Ed Small who was just opening a new place called Small's Paradise. He was having a hard time getting whiskey at a good price so he was interested and would look at it before the week was out. Things were looking up because I also wanted to play jazz at Small's.

When I got to *The Crisis* Tuesday morning, Mr. Dill was reading the newspaper. He was reading the *Daily Mirror* so I knew Dr. DuBois was not in yet.

"What do you find so amusing in that trashy paper?" Miss Fauset asked.

"Just the way some people can lie," Mr. Dill answered. "The city inspectors went to the Cotton Club to see if it can be reopened. You remember they were closed for liquor violation?"

"Go on," Miss Fauset said.

"Well, when they got to the club to inspect it for illegal booze they found an undisclosed number of illegal crates of bootleg whiskey on the premises!" Mr. Dill said, rubbing his hands together. "Let me read you this part. 'The police have arrested Mr. Owney Madden and charged him with fifty-four counts of illegal possession of alcoholic beverages, which could send him back to prison for as much as twenty years. Mr. Madden said he was framed and would take care of whoever has done this to him.' Can you imagine the nerve of these people?"

The Cotton Club? Bootleg whiskey? I suddenly felt very tired and put my head down on the desk. Miss Fauset asked if I was all right and I told her no, that I was not all right. She asked if I wanted her to take me to the hospital. That was just as the door opened and the first policeman came into the office.

I AM TAKEN TO JAIL LIKE A COMMON THUG, GIVEN THE THIRD DEGREE, BUT AM SAVED BY MY REPUTATION AS AN INTERNATIONAL GANGSTER, BAD MAN, AND THE NEW BREED OF CRIMINAL.

Miss Fauset was the first one to start crying in the office and I didn't mind that too much. What I did mind was just as the police were putting the handcuffs on me, the door opened and Langston Hughes walked in. His eyes bugged out and *scared* jumped all over his face.

"Mark!" he called out to me.

I wanted to say his name but the words just wouldn't come. A big policeman had me by the shoulder and was just about lifting me as he took me to the door.

I wanted to tell Langston that I was not really a bad person, that there had just been a chain of unfortunate circumstances that had put me in the position I found myself.

"I would appreciate it if the name of our organization was kept out of the papers," Dr. DuBois said.

"Are any of these people in your gang?" a tall policeman asked me, pointing me toward Langston.

"No, sir," I said.

People on 14th Street stopped and stared at me as I was led down the street to the police wagon. I was almost glad to step up into the back of the wagon but I felt terrible when the door slammed behind me. There was a grate in the back door, and I stood up and looked through it and saw that the busy people were going on about their business as I was going about the business of going to jail.

When I got to the 8th precinct station on East 22nd Street I was surprised to see that Fats was already there. He was sitting on a bench in the waiting area. The policeman who had me by the back of my collar marched me up to the high desk where a bigheaded sergeant with red hair sat having coffee.

"This is the one they say owns the liquor," he said, pushing me into the desk before releasing his grip on my collar. "They get younger and younger."

The desk sergeant took down my name and address and asked me what prisons I had been in.

"None, sir," I answered in a loud voice.

"That's good, son," he said. "So you won't be disappointed in any one we send you to, will you?"

I was scared out of my mind, especially when they had me holding a sign with my name and a number on it. By the time they led me through the swinging doors into the back rooms my knees were shaking and I would have given anything for a quick trip to the bathroom. There were dark figures in the cells I passed and a chill went through me. The uniformed officer pushed me into a room where three very big guys in plain clothes were yelling at Crab Cakes. One of them stood behind him and every time he gave them an answer they didn't like he would hit him in the back of the head.

"I didn't buy that whiskey!" Crab Cakes was ducking from the blow even before it came. "He's the one, officer. I swear it!"

"What's your name?" The detective pointed toward a chair and I sat on it.

"Mark Purvis," I said quickly.

"You one of Bumpy Johnson's hoods?"

"No, sir!"

The blow to the side of my head knocked me off the chair and I found myself sitting on the floor.

"Who told you to get off that chair?"

I got up as fast as I could and sat on the chair again.

"You one of Bumpy Johnson's hoods?"

"Yes, sir."

"He working for Mr. Schultz, too," Crab Cakes added.

"Get Fats in here."

One of the detectives went out and got Fats who came in with a handful of pork rinds.

"Fats, you have to straighten all this out," the detective who had hit Crab Cakes said. His tone with Fats was gentle, and Fats didn't look like he was worried at all. "Who does this kid work for?"

"Anybody who'll give him a couple of dollars," Fats said with a shrug. "Right now he's the one who owns all the liquor because nobody else wants to claim it. Ain't nobody want to go to jail over one little shipment. Not worth it. You want some pork rinds?"

"Nah, can't eat that stuff," the detective said. "You sure he don't work for Owney?"

"I don't think he does," Fats said. "But one never knows, do one?"

"They're not going to put him on trial," the detective who hit me said. "He's too small a fish. Let's just shoot him and turn him loose."

"But he can become a bigger fish," Fats said. "So why don't you keep that liquor as evidence? Then if he does anything else you can always bring it out and stick him in the Tombs or send him upstate to Sing Sing. He'll like the uniforms they have up there."

"We got to charge him with something," one of the detectives said.

Just then the door opened and a policeman said that my parents were outside with a lawyer from the National Association for the Advancement of Colored People.

"And the sergeant doesn't want this many Colored people in the precinct so he wants to know what are you going to do."

The biggest detective, the one that had been hitting Crab Cakes, took a deep breath and pulled his fist back as if he was going to punch him again. Crab Cakes ducked and all the policemen laughed at that.

"Fats, some of the boys are going to have a little party down at the club on Fourteenth Street. It's going to be from eight to about eleven next Friday night," the detective said. "Could be a fun thing. A few guys, a few young ladies. We could sure use a little music. You think you can drop by with a couple of boys and play for us?"

"Sure can," Fats said. He put on the biggest grin I had ever seen in my life. "If the joint can jump, I'll have it jumping."

"I'll give you my address," the detective said. "Get the rest of these miscreants out of here."

The sunshine out on 22nd Street was the prettiest I

have ever seen in my entire life. We walked across town to the West Side and got the A train up to Harlem.

Mama thanked Jesus all the way uptown and I was wondering if Jesus could have looked anything like Fats Waller. At home Mama had me on my knees praying for almost an hour. I was hoping that the Good Lord would forget about the whole thing and let me go on with my life. Mama mothered me with hugs after the praying and talked about how she was just glad I wasn't going to jail.

I couldn't get over Fats. He was waltzing around that police station like he owned it. He was big and he was smart, but that wasn't what it was all about. What it was about was that Fats could cook. He could play anything for anybody, and the whole world was waiting to hear him. Gangsters gave him slack. The police listened to him. Fats was Fats and that was that. Fats was what I wanted to get to, to be playing so good, and swinging so hard that the whole world took you serious. I thought maybe Fats was the newest Negro of all.

The next morning I came downstairs and found Henry on the stoop with a copy of the *Daily Mirror*.

"Man, you are in a white newspaper," he said. "It's on page four and continued on page fourteen," he said.

I sat down on the stoop next to Tim Kelly and read the story.

The New Negro

Our Colored population, especially those who live in Harlem, are talking about a New Negro, and one of the most notorious of these "New Negroes" is sixteen-year-old Mark Purvis. Purvis, a burly youth, is connected with the intrastate bootlegging ring that has ties to the notorious Owney Madden as well as to Dutch Schultz and a number of Negro policy dealers and reefer fiends. Purvis, also known as "Crab Killer Purvis" and "Mark the Shark," is suspected of crimes in New York, New Jersey, and Baltimore, Maryland.

"I don't mean anything personal or nothing," Henry said, "but my mom said I can't hang out with you anymore."

■ ■ ■ ■ ■ ■ ■ ■ ■ ■ ■ ■ ■ ■ ■ ■ ■ ■ ■

WHERE I LEARN THAT THERE ARE TWO SIDES OF FAMOUS STREET. THE SUNNY SIDE IS WHERE EVERYBODY SHAKES YOUR HAND. THE SHADY SIDE IS WHERE EVERY-BODY GIVES YOU THE FISH EYE. STILL, SLOWLY BUT SURELY, I SEE THAT I AM GETTING BACK TO BEING THE OLD ME.

■ ■ ■ ■ ■ ■ ■ ■ ■ ■ ■ ■ ■ ■ ■ ■ ■ ■ ■

I got to the barbershop at two minutes to five and grabbed my number. On Friday evening you had to be at the shop by 5:00 to get the fifty-cent haircut. If you got there after 5:00 Ralph, the guy who owned the barbershop, would charge you a whole seventy-five cents.

"Hey, ain't you the young man was in the paper?" A dark-skinned man wearing overalls pointed at me with the biggest finger I have ever seen. "You big-time, right?"

"Just going from day to day," I said. "Trying to pull my own weight."

"Got your picture in the newspaper, too," the man said. "Lord Almighty! Now every cop you see is going to know who you are. Every time somebody sneeze in Harlem they're going to be looking in your direction."

"How many copies of the paper your mama buy so she can show her friends how you such a big-time celebrity?" Earl Joshua, who owned the antique shop, had turned his chair around and leaned on the back as he spoke. "Maybe you can even get it printed in the church bulletin, right next to the offering prayer for the week."

"Y'all leave that young man alone," Ralph said, sharpening his razor on the strap next to the chair. "He ain't bad, just a little lazy. He figured it was too much trouble to go out looking for trouble so he got his picture in the paper so trouble can come to him. You can't get that kind of free advertising unless you're big-time."

I put my number back up on the rack and was headed out the door when Big Finger called out to me. "Hey, gangster, you going out to shoot somebody?"

"I'm not a gangster," I said. "And you don't have to get on my case like that."

"Mark, when you're playing with fire you've got to deal with the heat," Ralph said. "And fire ain't particular about who it burns."

It seemed that everybody in New York had read the *Daily Mirror* and seen my picture in it. Old women who never spoke to me came up and said hello. One woman with her hair up in curlers said that I should be ashamed of myself.

"Your mother didn't raise you to be no hoodlum," she said.

It was funny in a way because I knew I wasn't a hood-lum, or at least I thought I wasn't, but I was getting to be pretty famous. Randy came around and started talking to me again and that was funny, too, because he hadn't wanted to be my friend when he thought I might be a criminal but now that the paper had said I was and had printed my picture he got to liking the idea. One person who didn't like the idea was Bumpy Johnson. I was walking along 125th Street and stopped in front of the Apollo to see who was going to be appearing there when Bumpy came up next to me.

"I got a message for you from Queenie," he said, half-way under his breath. "It's from me, too. You listening?"

"Yeah," I answered. My heart was beating kind of fast but I was listening hard.

"Queenie said you don't owe her nothing," Bumpy said. "You just keep your distance. Anybody gets their pictures in the white papers is nothing but trouble. So you just stay on your side of the street from now on. You got that?"

"Sure."

"Queenie is going to chase Dutch Schultz out of the numbers business," Bumpy said. "And if you try to mus-cle in anywhere above 126th Street all the way to 148th Street and the river, I personally will plant you six feet deep and water your grave twice a day to see if you grow. You got that?"

"I got it."

When Bumpy left, it took a full two minutes before my knees stopped shaking. As I walked uptown I noticed the air was a little cooler and it felt like the end of summer. When I got to my stoop, Mr. Mills and Tim Kelly were playing checkers.

"Here comes Mr. Big-Time," Thomas Mills said. "I heard they going to put his picture on the newsreel and show him off at the movies."

"This old boy got more contacts than the mayor himself." Tim Kelly made a move but kept his finger on the checker so he could take it back.

"He's hotter than a two-dollar pistol," Mr. Mills said. He watched as Tim took his hand off the checker, then took two of his men. "He needs to buy himself a white hat. Then all the would-be little gangsters can spot him easy. You know, the best way to make a reputation for yourself is to shoot a celebrity."

"Thanks for the encouragement," I said.

"I can see your tombstone now." Mr. Mills looked up in the sky as if he was seeing something.

> "Here lies old Mark
> Known for his notoriety
> Got shot four times
> And that will last him for all eternity!"

"That's got a real ring to it," said Tim. "It really do."

I went upstairs and thought about what the men in the barbershop and the people in the neighborhood were saying about me. They were kidding around some, but I knew that for the first time in my life people were looking at me and not liking what they were seeing.

It took Labor Day nearly all summer to show up but when it did it was a scorcher. I could see the heat rising from the sidewalks. People were lying out on their fire escapes, and the people whose awnings worked had them pulled out. Mr. Lee, who worked at the racetrack, had put a piece of ice on his fire escape, covered it with a piece of burlap, and laid his head right on it.

Mama was still rolling her eyes toward heaven every time she saw me but otherwise things were cooling down. I knew she was thinking about Matt leaving later in the day. The whole family, plus Henry and Lavinia, went on the Labor Day picnic with the Ezekiel A.M.E. Church in Morningside Park. At the picnic, there was a huge pot of mullet stew, piles of crispy-fried butterfish and soft-shell crabs, spareribs, and mountains of potato salad, collards, curried rice, and baked yams. The smells alone would have injured a weak man.

Mama said she heard that Morningside Presbyterian, on the corner of 122nd Street and Morningside Avenue, was going to be bought by the Church of the Master, a black congregation. She said she didn't know where all those black people were coming from. Reverend McKinnon, from Ezekiel, said that if you paved the streets with gold, people would come, and that we were painting Harlem with black dignity, which was even better than gold. I liked that.

Uncle Cephus had come to the park, and Mama told everybody how he was helping Matt go to Storer College down at Harpers Ferry, West Virginia. That's when he broke the bad news to Mama. He had thought it over and had decided that I was not the kind of young man fit to become his assistant in the House of Palms undertaking business. Mama took me to one side and said that was the result of me hanging around with criminals.

Thank God for Bumpy Johnson.

All the time we were in the park, eating and talking, and sometimes singing hymns, I was thinking about Matt leaving. Uncle Cephus was going to lend us the money to send him to school for a year and we were going to pay him back by the week. Mama was talking about taking in a boarder and having me sleep on the couch, but Daddy said he wasn't going to have no strange man living in his house, and Mama wasn't going to have no woman, so that settled that and I get the whole room to myself.

After the picnic we went home and Matt finished packing. Mama was nervous, and I saw her wiping at her eyes. Matt's train was going to leave at 7:15 from Pennsylvania Station and when we went downstairs some of the neighbors said good-bye to him and wished him luck. Tim Kelly was sitting on a milk crate and he got up and came over to shake Matt's hand. He said the race needed young men like Matt, and that when he died he was going to be happy to know that there were college men to take his place in the struggle. Well, what did he say that for? Mama started boohooing all over the place, as I figured she would.

Pennsylvania Station was a magical place to me, with people rushing around, redcaps pushing handcarts stacked high with luggage, and the big boards announcing all the trains and where they were going. Most of the redcaps were black, but all people, black and white, waited in the same huge room. When Matt's train was announced, me and Daddy took his bags downstairs. A porter looked at Matt's tickets and told him which car to get into. People were milling about the station, saying their good-byes, kissing and crying, and getting set to move on with their lives. The train, dark and sleek, looked like some kind of big animal just waiting to take off.

Mama hugged Matt, and Daddy shook his hand and then he hugged him, too. He told him to mind he didn't get too big for his business, and Matt said he wouldn't. Then Lavinia kissed Matt and started boo-hooing and then stood posing next to Mama.

Matt put his arm around my shoulders and we walked up to the train together.

"Mark, you have to leave the streets out there where they're lying," Matt said. "Don't bring them into the house. Mama can't deal with it and I don't want to see you dealing with them. You got some smarts, little brother. It's up to you to use them."

"I can deal," I said. "You go on and save the world."

"I don't know if I can save the world or not," Matt said. "I'm just not sure. But I know it's going to be harder for me if things aren't right back home."

"I'll keep them right," I said.

I had never heard Matt say he wasn't sure of himself before and it surprised me. Then we were shaking hands and he was throwing his suitcases up on the train, and jumping on. He disappeared for a while and then Daddy saw him at one of the windows and pointed him out. Matt waved at us as the train seemed to come to life and started rolling out of the station. It moved slowly at first, jerkily, then seemed to gather itself up and went roaring into the darkness of the tunnel.

We walked over to the IRT and took the subway uptown. All the way we were quiet. When we got out at

125th Street, and Lavinia had left, Daddy put his arm around Mama's shoulder and said, "Ginny, we done good."

Miss Fauset sent me a letter saying that Dr. DuBois would give me a good recommendation even though I had associated with the criminal element. I figured she must have grabbed him and twisted his arm behind his back to get it. I would have loved to see that. She also said I would get a free subscription to *The Crisis*, which I did not want, because I had decided once and for all that I did not want to be a New Negro, or a criminal, or an undertaker. I was going to open my own club and be the leader of the house band that would feature me and Henry and Randy, if he practiced more.

The second day after school, I was walking out of the door with Henry and who was waiting outside with his collar turned up and a new dog on a leash?

"I got a job out near Hoboken this weekend," Crab Cakes said, his foot up on the dashboard of a black-and-gray Packard. It was some sharp. "Fats is working so he can't come. All we got to do is pick up some goods for the Clara Smith Club. It's easy money, man."

"I didn't hear nothing!" Henry walked away with his hands in the air. "I didn't hear nothing!"

"Come on," Crab Cakes was saying. "We could use the money. You like good music and all the blues singers work out at Clara's place. Fats would have come if he wasn't working. I can even talk to Clara about you working there sometime."

For a minute I felt myself getting excited, wanting to go with Crab Cakes, to climb into the back of the Packard and feel my heart racing.

"I don't think so," I said. "Got too many things to do."

"Where you going to get money this easy?" Crab Cakes asked. "Won't take that long to do, either."

"No, but thanks for asking," I said.

Crab Cakes looked disappointed, but he shrugged it off, and opened the door for his new dog. In a way I was disappointed, too. I knew that somewhere inside I had wanted to go. But then I had thought about how Ralph and the guys in the barbershop had looked at me, how they had started talking about me as if I was somebody different than I had thought about myself. And I thought about Langston saying that there was more than one kind of real, that the kind of real at the rent party had been hot and swinging and seemed like the only way to live, but that there were other faces and other places that I would find just as real.

I didn't know what I wanted to do with myself. I knew I didn't want to be an undertaker and I knew I didn't want to get arrested every weekend, but that's about where it ended. I did know I wanted to be in Harlem, though. I wanted to be around the music and all the people. The

New Negroes as well as the old ones. I loved them all. I loved the summer on Lenox Avenue when it wasn't too hot and the winter if the wind coming down from Sugar Hill wasn't too cold. I loved sitting on the stoop with Old Man Mills and sitting in the Lafayette listening to Fats wail on the organ. That was my kind of life, even though I hadn't sorted out all the particulars just yet.

A few drops fell but the sidewalk just cooked it up so you couldn't even tell it was raining. Down the street a man with a horse and wagon was selling watermelons and fresh vegetables.

I saw Henry and caught up with him.

"You back in the bootleg business?" he asked.

"Not unless it's bootlegging watermelons," I said. "You think you could get in on that?"

"I guess so." Henry smiled. "As long as none of them get killed. It's a pitiful thing to see a watermelon shot up."

Real People and Places in
Harlem Summer

ABYSSINIAN BAPTIST CHURCH
The church moved from midtown Manhattan to West 138th Street in Harlem in 1923. For many years, it was the most influential church in Harlem.

ANDERSON, MARIAN (1897–1993) Classical singer who made numerous recordings; won a vocal contest sponsored by the New York Philharmonic in 1925 and became the first African American to sing with the famous Metropolitan Opera.

BATTLE, SAMUEL (1883–1966)
One of the first black policemen on the New York City force.

CONNIE'S INN First a delicatessen, then a popular Harlem nightclub on 131st Street near the Lafayette Theater. Fats Waller worked at Connie's Inn as a delivery boy.

COTTON CLUB Built circa 1918 on 142nd Street and Lenox Avenue. Bought by mob boss Owney Madden in 1923, it became the predominant club in Harlem during Prohibition, bringing black bands and acts to white patrons.

COVARRUBIAS, MIGUEL (1904–1957) Mexican artist whose caricatures captured the leading figures of the Harlem Renaissance. His book, *Negro Drawings*, is an enduring classic of the period.

CULLEN, COUNTEE (1903–1946) A poet and scholar, his first book of poetry, *Color*, was published in 1925. He married the daughter of W. E. B. DuBois.

DUBOIS, WILLIAM EDWARD BURGHARDT (1868–1963) Outstanding sociologist and intellectual, and one of the founders of the National Association for the Advancement of Colored People (NAACP). He was the editor of *The Crisis* and a leading force in black intellectual life.

DURANTE, JIMMY (1893–1980)
American comedian and singer.

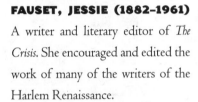

FAUSET, JESSIE (1882–1961)
A writer and literary editor of *The Crisis*. She encouraged and edited the work of many of the writers of the Harlem Renaissance.

FLEGENHEIMER, ARTHUR, AKA DUTCH SCHULTZ (1902–1935)
A leading bootlegger, Dutch Schultz also ran much of the illegal numbers racket in Harlem. Like most local hoodlums, he also had a legitimate moving business.

HARLEM RENS An early New York–based basketball team.

HOLSTEIN, CASPAR (1877–1944) Real estate tycoon, businessman, and a major illegal numbers banker. He also sponsored literary contests that were run by *Opportunity* magazine.

HUGHES, LANGSTON (1902–1967) The best-known and most widely published writer of the Harlem Renaissance. Hughes published short stories, autobiographies, nonfiction, plays, and children's books, as well as newspaper columns and translations. "The Negro Speaks of Rivers," one of his most famous poems, was first published in *The Crisis*.

JOHNSON, ELLSWORTH RAYMOND, AKA "BUMPY" JOHNSON (1906–1968) Originally from South Carolina, Bumpy always carried a gun and a knife and made it clear that he was more than willing to use both. Often worked with Queenie St. Clair.

KNOPF, ALFRED (1892–1984) Published much of the material that introduced Harlem to the world, including *The Weary Blues* by Langston Hughes and *Negro Drawings* by Miguel Covarrubias.

LAFAYETTE THEATER Located at 132nd Street and Seventh Avenue; supported theater pieces and reviews, and showed films.

MCKINNEY, NINA MAE (1909–1967) A beautiful young singer and actress. She appeared in *Blackbirds of 1928* on Broadway and in 1929 appeared in the film *Hallelujah*. One of the first black movie stars.

MADDEN, OWNEY (1892–1965) Bought the Club Deluxe in 1923 from boxer Jack Johnson and reopened it as the Cotton Club.

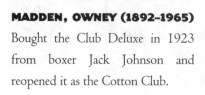

NEWSOME, EFFIE LEE (1885–1979) Children's editor for *The Crisis*. A librarian at Central State College and Wilberforce University in Ohio, she dedicated her life to bringing poetry to African-American culture.

PACE, HARRY (1884–1943) Music publisher, recorder, and owner of Black Swan Records, the first black-owned record company. He recorded Ethel Waters and Trixie Smith.

POWELL, REVEREND ADAM CLAYTON, SR. (1865–1953) Named pastor of the Abyssinian Baptist Church in 1908. Reverend Powell turned the church into a vital community organization.

POWELL, REVEREND ADAM CLAYTON, JR. (1908–1972) Succeeded his father as pastor of the Abyssinian Baptist Church in 1937. Was elected to Congress in 1945 and was the first influential African American in Congress since the Reconstruction.

RENAISSANCE BALLROOM AND CASINO The first floor of the Renaissance was dedicated to dining and nightclub acts. The second

floor was for dances and, occasionally, basketball games.

SMALL'S PARADISE Ed Small, building on the success of the Sugar Cane Club, opened Small's Paradise in October 1925.

SMITH, TRIXIE (1895–1921) Blues singer who started with Black Swan Records and later moved on to an outstanding career as a singer and recording artist.

ST. CLAIR, STEPHANIE, AKA QUEENIE (dates unknown) A black Frenchwoman from Martinique. Queenie ran an extortion racket and challenged Dutch Schultz for control of the Harlem numbers racket.

THURMAN, WALLACE (1902–1934) Best known as a novelist, he was the editor of *Fire: Devoted to Younger Negro Artists*, and a nonfiction work on Harlem.

VAN VECHTEN, CARL (1880–1964) Introduced many black writers to white publishers. Also a noted photographer. Van Vechten took this self-portrait as well as the photo of Langston Hughes on page 158.

WALKER, A'LELIA (1885–1931)
The daughter of Madame C.J. Walker, the first black female millionaire. A'lelia was known for her lavish parties, extravagant lifestyle, and support of the arts in Harlem.

WALLER, THOMAS "FATS" (1904–1943) His father was a deacon and, later, pastor of the Abyssinian Baptist Church in Harlem. Fats first worked professionally as an organist at the Lafayette and Lincoln theaters in 1923. During his short lifetime, he recorded such bestsellers as "Honeysuckle Rose" and "Ain't Misbehavin'" as well as classical music. One of the most brilliant and well-known musicians of his time, Fats died shortly before his fortieth birthday.

WASHINGTON, BOOKER T. (1856–1915) Black educator who accepted the idea of blacks having positions in society separate from whites in return for the gains offered by education. He hoped for a gradual recognition of black worth by whites, a position that W. E. B. DuBois loathed.

WATERS, ETHEL (1896–1977) Singer and actress. Recorded with Black Swan Records and appeared in *Jump Steady* in 1919 at the Lafayette Theater.

■ ■

Photo Credits

Abyssinian Baptist Church: New York Public Library/Art Resource, NY

Anderson, Marion: The Art Archive/Culver Pictures, NY

Battle, Samuel: © Bettmann/Corbis, NY

Cotton Club: Frank Driggs Collection, NY

Covarrubias, Miguel: The Granger Collection, NY

Cullen, Countee: Yale Collection of American Literature,
The Beinecke Rare Book and Manuscript Library, CT.

Dubois, William Edward Burghardt: The New York Public Library/Art
Resource, NY

Durante, Jimmy: © Bettmann/Corbis, NY

Fauset, Jessie: © Corbis, NY

Flegenheimer, Arthur, AKA Dutch Schultz: © Bettmann/Corbis, NY

Harlem Rens: © James Van Der Zee, NY

Holstein, Caspar: © Bettmann/Corbis, NY

Hughes, Langston: © Carl Van Vechten/The Van Vechten Trust/ National
Portrait Gallery, Smithsonian Institution/Art Resource/ Gravure and
Compilation © Eakins Press Foundation,NY

Knopf, Alfred: © Bettmann/Corbis, NY

■ ■

Walter Dean Myers grew up in Harlem and now lives in Jersey City, New Jersey. A beloved and outstanding author of children's and young adult literature, his many awards include two Newbery Honors, five Coretta Scott King Awards, and the Michael J. Printz Award. His most recent books for Scholastic Press include *The Beast* and *A Time to Love: Stories from the Old Testament.*

■ ■

23